A SPARK OF BLUE FLAME

BY

SANDRA STANLEY-STONE

Strategic Book Publishing
New York, New York

Copyright © 2009

All rights reserved – Sandra Stanley-Stone

No part of this book may be reproduced or transmitted in any form or by any means, graphic, electronic, or mechanical, including photocopying, recording, taping, or by any information storage retrieval system, without the permission, in writing, from the publisher.

Strategic Book Publishing
An imprint of Writers Literary & Publishing Services, Inc.
845 Third Avenue, 6th Floor – 6016
New York, NY 10022
http://www.strategicbookpublishing.com

ISBN: 978-1-60860-630-6

Printed in the United States of America

Book Design: Bonita S. Watson

CONTENTS

Prologue . . . . *vii*
Chapter 1 1
Chapter 2 5
Chapter 3 9
Chapter 4 13
Chapter 5 19
Chapter 6 25
Chapter 7 31
Chapter 8 37
Chapter 9 47
Chapter 10. 55
Chapter 11. 61
Chapter 12. 65
Chapter 13. 71
Chapter 14. 75
Chapter 15. 77
Chapter 16. 83
Chapter 17. 85
Chapter 18. 93
Chapter 19. 101
Chapter 20. 105

Chapter 21 111
Chapter 22 115
Chapter 23 117
Chapter 24 121
Chapter 25 127
Chapter 26 131
Chapter 27 135
Chapter 28 139
Chapter 29 147
Chapter 30 149
Chapter 31 151
Chapter 32 155
Chapter 33 157
Chapter 34 159
Chapter 35 161
Chapter 36 163
Chapter 37 165
Chapter 38 167
Chapter 39 171
Chapter 40 173
Epilogue *179*

*"All torment, trouble, wonder, and amazement
Inhibits here. Some heavenly power guide us
Out of this fearful country!"*

Shakespeare: Tempest. I

PROLOGUE

THE FIRST BOOK OF BELANOS, THE BEGINNING

Lord Dagda, All Father, Provider, God of Good, created the cosmos and formed the Worlds, which he strung together like jeweled beads on a necklace of silver-blue Energy Links and, in His wisdom, called the Strand of Life. Lord Dagda then set upon each World Man made in His image and Woman made in the image of His Beloved Goddess, Lady Brighid.

Proudly, Lord Dagda said, "I place the Strand of Life around your neck, so that you may hold my people near your heart for safekeeping during all eternity."

Lord Dagda saw the Strand of Life sparkling like an array of diamonds against her skin and knew that she would nurture and love His creation and His people as she loved Him.

But, Loche, Evil Incarnate, God of Chaos, loathed Lord Dagda and hated all.

Soon, Lord Dagda and Lady Brighid conceived and bore a son, who was named Belanos. And when their son had grown like unto a man, Lady Brighid to her husband said, "Now Belanos shall inherit the Strand of Life." And so saying, she placed the Strand of Life into Belanos' hand to love Lord Dagda's creation, for Belanos, strong of spirit, would shield the people from all Evil.

And Belanos took the Strand of Life and placed it around his own neck for safekeeping, and His Lord and Father knew that Belanos would nurture and love His creation and His people as Belanos loved his own Father.

But Loche, Evil Incarnate, God of Chaos, loathed Lord Dagda and hated all.

Then Loche, desiring to destroy Lord Dagda's good creation and His people, crept through the night into Belanos' bed chamber. While he slept, Loche ripped the chain of the Strand of Life from its Keeper. The Strand of Life broke, and the jeweled beads of Earth and Wry fell to the floor.

Lord and Lady Dagda, both All-knowing, stepped into the chamber to take Loche prisoner. Lady Brighid picked up the jewels of Earth and Wry still joined by their Energy Link from the floor, and held them in the palm of Her hand. Lord Dagda twisted together an Energy Link to form a Twisted Plane, where He banished Loche to walk its never-ending circuit forever.

Then Lord Dagda shrunk the Twisted Plane into a minuscule circle of silver, placed it into a Jeweled Locket hanging from a golden chain, locked it with the Key of K'vle, and beckoned the One-Horne of Wry to Him and said, "I charge you to forever wear the Jeweled Locket and keep it from Evil Hands." With this onus, the One-Horne returned to Wry. Lady Brighid took the Strand of Life without the jewels of Earth and Wry, joined it together by the broken blue-silver Energy Links, and placed it around Belanos' neck. Returning with Lord Dagda to their room, she gently set the jewels of Earth and Wry on her bedside table upon a black-velvet cushion called Cosmos.

And trudging along the Twisted Plane, Loche, God of Chaos, spent an eternity plotting his revenge.

CHAPTER ONE

OPEN THE GATE BETWEEN THE WORLDS, BEWARE EVIL BEYOND THE VEIL.

Tapping a fingernail impatiently upon the ancient, carved tiny leather book in his lap, Kylasar peered into the fireplace, his obsidian eyes reflecting fire within the smoldering ashes. He felt at ease in this windowless stone-walled room with its marble floors and high ceiling. Here in his sanctuary, leather-bound books, odd-shaped jars filled with murky liquids, and topaz, malachite, moonstone, and onyx gemstones littered shelves set against the walls. On the work table cluttered with books and parchments, candles, spilling the smell of cinnamon into the air, melted into stumps like fat orange and yellow toads.

Kylasar breathed in the odor, feeling his magical power grow stronger. He had spent years searching for spells, cantrips, and gramaryes to help him gain more power, and now in this small book he had finally found a ritual to call Loche, the God of Chaos. Surely, if he could contact Loche, the god would grant him more power. Kylasar stood with book in hand and collected from his work table black, red, and green powders, brushes, cloth, a silver chalice, and stiletto for the ritual. After kicking dusty books, papers, and junk to the sides of the room, he dumped all onto the smooth flagstone area in the middle of the floor. On his knees, Kylasar picked up the book, flipped to the earmarked page of the ritual's design, and with green powder began painting a large square on the floor, referring to the illustration time and again. He turned for the vial of black powder.

Later, when he drew back to observe his handiwork, he saw that the green square had black curlicues intersecting and wrapping each side. Already faint yellow nodes of energy glowed inside each corner of the design. He could feel the hair on his arms rising from the gathering of magical power and grew excited.

He set down the black powder. Picking up a vial of red powder and holding up his robe so its hem would not break the design, he carefully stepped over the green and black powder outside the square where he drew in red powder all but the last six inches of a large circle six feet across, surrounding the green square. He stepped through the opening to stand outside the design and was pleased that he could not see any major difference between his work and the illustration.

Following the ritual instructions, he softly said,

"With this I open a portal to the Twisted Plane, where Loche, God of Chaos reigns!"

Removing his robe and shirt, Kylasar sat cross-legged on the floor directly in front of the break in the circle. With a leather thong, he tied back his long dark-red hair.

Kylasar placed the silver chalice on the floor in front of his crossed ankles. From the floor, he took the silver stiletto and held its pearl handle in his right hand. He laid the stiletto's razor-sharp blade against the tender skin between his wrist and elbow. He closed his eyes, and speaking the old language clearly and precisely, he moved the blade across and into the skin. As the blood began to flow from the wound, he opened his eyes and turned his arm to fill the silver chalice. When it was full, he circled the wounded arm with a strip of cloth, knotted it with his good hand, and pulled it tight with his teeth. Only then did he allow himself to relax.

Once again, he carefully moved into the circle to place the blood-filled chalice inside the red powder, within the center of the black-trellised green-powder square. He stepped out, bent down, and with the bloodied tip of the blade, drew the red powder circle shut behind him.

He walked around the red circle to stand at the top of the northern side of the green square. *Now,* he thought, *for the truly dangerous part.*

"Loche!" he called, his voice echoing from the walls. "Hear me, Kylasar, who commands you. Come!"

At his words, a shaft of green-tinged yellow light stretched from each corner of the square to form a fifteen-foot-high pyramid. When the shafts of light touched at its apex, sparks shot upward into a dome of golden, dazzling light, which transformed into a cage of golden light twenty feet high with its bottom six feet across touching the red powder. Filaments of golden light pulsed and crisscrossed the surface of the cage until Kylasar had to shade his eyes from overbearing brightness. The golden filaments, like laser optics, turned orange then orange-red then red hot, melting the edge of the golden cage and soldered it to the flagstone floor. Kylasar felt as if his skin would burn to cinders, but within nanoseconds, the red blaze softened to tiny lines of light flickering across the now almost-invisible surface of the cage.

Inside the cage and just beneath the surface of the dome, two huge eyes looked at Kylasar with such intensity that he shrank back, terrified at what he'd just accomplished. Loche's face, like skinless bone, glowed like verdigris on copper, reflected light from the dome and his lidless, slitted cat-like yellow-green eyes glowed eerily. The god curled his fanged mouth into a leer. His ribs were visible through transparent green-tinged scaled skin, his arms were jointed like an insect's leg, and his long, thin fingers curved, like black, razor-sharp talons. His legs were back-jointed with a sharp spur that curved up on the back of each toward his calf, and his feet had hooves. His green head, like a cobra mesmerizing his prey, moved sinuously side to side. The god opened his mouth, and cringing, Kylasar imagined a mouth that size could swallow him whole.

"You called?"

Kylasar shivered. Something this terrifying could swat him way like a dragon batting at a mosquito. But, as long as he had performed the ritual's incantation correctly and precisely, Loche could not escape from the cage. Silently applauding his brilliance to kowtow a god, Kylasar bravely stepped forward and lifted his head to look Loche eye to eye.

"I have brought you an offering, Loche," he stated carelessly pointing to the silver chalice inside the cage on the floor at the feet of the god. Loche bent down, picked up the chalice like a tiny thimble between huge fingers, and tossed the entire vessel with its blood offering down his throat. His eyes flamed.

"What do you want, puny human?"

"I want to destroy the Blue Sorcerers."

"What do I reap from such a project?"

"Whatever you want!" Kylasar replied, his eagerness slipping out, although he had not wanted to appear impatient.

Loche snapped his head to its height and opened his mouth, with its layers of needle-sharp teeth, and roared. Green flames spewed forth, and the heat buffeted Kylasar; he stepped back, warily eyeing the floor to make sure the circle held.

"Erase the circle!" Loche thundered.

"What do you want?" Kylasar asked.

Loche's roar whipped the air into a gale that forced Kylasar to his knees. He wondered if this time he had gone too far, had summoned something he would not be able to control. Before he could draw another breath, coldness touched the back of his neck and, like a needle pricking his skin, sending chilled ice, like a serpent slithering down his spine, up into his mind.

He struggled to shake off the mind control, but ice cold, fanged thoughts froze his own. The coldness grabbed control of his muscles and marched him like a marionette to the edge of the cage. He watched in horror as his leg rose slowly and kicked at the bottom of the cage where it sat atop the red powder. His leg kicked the cage, the magical spell broke, the cage turned back into light fiber optics, the red powder scattered into dust motes. Kylasar felt his head jerk backward and saw Loch leering into his eyes. The god suddenly dissolved into a putrescent, bile-colored vapor that poured across the flagstone floor, wrapped around Kylasar's legs, slithered around his body like a snake, then infiltrated his host's mind and body like a parasite.

Kylasar tried to scream while Loche laughed aloud. *Now I own your body and mind!* Loche's words reverberated within Kylasar's mind. *Once my body is free, then I will destroy the Blue Sorcerers and their God and Goddess, Lord Dagda and Lady Brighid. Revenge will finally be mine!*

CHAPTER TWO

POWERS OF AIR UNLOCK WRY'S GATE, BLESS THE KEY OF K'VLE.

On her way home after a week of searching for her ten-year-old daughter, Katherine Kylasar blinked back tears to watch her car's headlights tunnel through the summer night. When her ex-husband, Eric, had failed to bring Amanda home after his weekend visitation, Katherine had reported her daughter missing to the police and had talked to Eric's neighbors, boss, and landlady. No one knew where he had gone. At the bus station and airport, she had shown a picture of her daughter to everyone who would listen. No one had seen Mandy. And now she had nowhere else to turn, nowhere else to look. For the tenth time that day, she bit her lip to keep back the tears.

The road, a two-lane blacktop, edged a lake where Katherine had passed a marina and bait shop some time back. Now the road curved to the right with silhouettes of black trees on either side rising against a dark gray starless sky.

Above the glow from the headlights, a bolt of lightning flashed blue and a crash of thunder reverberated against her ears. Katherine shuddered and tightened her grip on the steering wheel. She rubbed a palm across a tear-streaked cheek. She had not seen any signs of habitation since the bait shop, and when a sign advertised a motel ahead, she slowed down to watch for the turnoff.

Again jagged lightning colored the night sky and electricity crackled in the air. The treetops to her right suddenly pulsated and brightened with an eerie blue light that flared into blinding streaks of white. Unable to see, she slammed on the brakes, slid into loose gravel on the side of the road, and shut her eyes. She smelled ionization mixed with moisture and opened her eyes slowly, blinking, wondering how close she had come to being struck by lightning. The bolt must have landed in the trees next to the roadside.

In the headlight's yellow glow, scraggly bushes looked like dark, huddling gnomes. Flickering above the headlights in a tree was a tiny blue-white flame. *From the lightning?* Katherine wondered. Wind chimes tinkled in the breeze. *Surely,* she thought, *there must be a house nearby.*

"Katherine!" a voice called softly. Maybe the lightning had damaged her hearing. She rolled the window down and heard again the faint tinkle of wind chimes. The tiny blue light spun and sparkled in the air, damp and cool, smelling of fish. Crickets chirped.

"Mandy needs you!" a voice whispered.

She peered into the tunnel of headlights looking for the person who owned the voice. But there was only the little flame of blue light. *I'm mentally exhausted,* she thought, *so it's not surprising that I hear strange voices telling me that Mandy needs me.* She felt tears well up and then reached to put the car in reverse. She had to keep going. Mandy needed her mother. The wind chimes grew louder and now Katherine froze. The little blue light was above the car's dark blue hood, dancing, leaving traces of reflected light like streamers from a Fourth of July sparkler.

"Katherine! Mandy needs you!"

The wind chime music spilled into the night air. *Had the voice come from the little light? Impossible!* Katherine turned away from the dancing flame to look through the window on her left. No one was there. She glanced in the rearview mirror and through the window on her right. Again, no one. But now the flame flickered on the windshield directly in front of her, like a heartbeat pulsing steadily, darkening to indigo, flashing to white, darkening to cobalt, flashing to white, deepening to French blue, flashing to white, then returning to indigo.

"Hurry! Mandy needs you!"

Without a doubt, she thought, *the voice is coming from the blue flame. But how could that be?* She shoved the gear shift into park and shut the engine off. The blue flame danced atop the windshield wipers.

"Where is Mandy?" Katherine asked and immediately decided she was crazy to be talking to a strange blue light dancing on her car in the middle of the night.

"Follow me!" the flame whispered, then whisked up into the air, flew to the edge of the tree line and hovered, seeming to wait for her.

Weird, she thought and wondered if the stress of looking for Mandy had pushed her over the brink. But if she were imagining this, would it hurt to follow the blue flame? Maybe not, but it would take time, and the longer Eric kept Mandy away from her, the harder it would be to find their trail. But the trail was already cold. Nonexistent. If the blue flame could lead her to Mandy, then she would be a fool not to follow.

Katherine took her flashlight from the glove box and slammed the car door behind her. She beamed the flashlight toward the trees to follow the little blue light flickering through the darkness. At a break in the foliage, she ducked her head under spindly black low-hanging branches and scrambled down a small incline. Wary of the eerie shadows that lengthened and shortened with the flashlight's movement, she paused mid-stride and wondered what she was doing chasing a will-o-the-wisp in a dark woods late at night. Surely, she thought, walking in a strange woods at night was not the act of a sane person. She turned to go and the wind chimes tinkled and the blue flame flew back to where she stood. "Mandy needs you!" its small voice said, "Hurry!" and the spark of blue spun away into the dark.

How could she doubt her ears and eyes? She had to believe that she would find Mandy, no matter how strange the means. Katherine stepped cautiously forward and walked deeper into the woods, afraid to turn back for fear of losing the little flame.

When the blue light hovered just ahead of her, Katherine stopped. *Now what?* she wondered. The blue flame flickered and tinkled and chimed frantically. She heard water lapping and a few feet from her, the flashlight's beam reflected off a gently rippling surface of a pool. Near the water's edge, she saw a sparkle of gold in a crack in a cleft of rock.

Leaning over for a closer look, she saw a small key, like one she had used to tighten her roller skates years ago. She knelt to remove the key. It felt cold and wet, and feeling the key coming free, Katherine jerked her hand up too quickly. Losing her balance and slipping on wet rock, she tumbled into the water.

    The cold took her breath away, and she felt herself sinking. She straightened her body so that when her feet touched the bottom of the pool, she could push herself up to the surface. But the pool was deeper than she had expected, and, seconds later, she still had not touched bottom. Realizing that she could not hold her breath much longer, Katherine tried kicking up to the surface; then she felt a white hot pain in her chest. The water seemed to solidify around her. For one terrified second, she saw herself trapped like a fly in a cube of plastic. *I'm going to die,* she thought. Unconsciousness sucked her into darkness.

CHAPTER THREE

DARKNESS SEES WHERE EVIL LURKS, BEHIND THE MIRROR, SCRYING.

From the work table, Kylasar picked up a pewter cup filled with wine, sat down, and drank deeply. Bevel, the Captain of the Guard, fidgeted nearby.

"Your Bevel is incompetent," Loche said. *"Worthless and better off dead."* Since invading Kylasar's mind ten years before, Loche had left Kylasar almost no time for his own thoughts. Kylasar wished Loche would cease his constant maledictions. He had tried to find some magic spell to remove the god's presence, but failing time after time, Kylasar realized that Loche knew everything he knew. And when Loche had discovered eating anything alive that crunched or scuttled made Kylasar vomit, Kylasar had learned very quickly to leave Loche alone. He supposed he should be thankful that Loche had given him control of his own body, but, after all, Kylasar supposed the god did not want to destroy his host's body until another became available. Angrily Kylasar hurled the pewter cup into the fireplace, watching sparks cascade across the flagstones. He forced his thoughts back to the Captain. "How could you lose sight of an animal?" He glared at Bevel. "There are only so many places a One-Horne can hide."

If he did not find the accursed animal soon, Kylasar's plan for destroying the Blue Sorcerers would be ruined. *"You mean my plan, human."*

Kylasar winced, tired of listening to the god. But Loche was right. It had been his plan. According to the ancient writings, the One-Horne wore a Jeweled Locket with Loche's corporeal body trapped inside on the Twisted Plane. And the only one who could get the Jeweled Locket from the One-Horne was an Earth Childe born of a Rhu'dammen Sorcerer. His daughter Amanda. That's the only reason he had gone to Earth, to that vile place with no magic, and had married Katherine. Now ten years had been wasted, years when he could have pushed the Blue Sorcerers back to Earth. Or into an early grave, which he preferred. He had to help release the demon body of Loche from the Twisted Plane. The more quickly the One-Horne was found, the sooner Kylasar would have his own body back. Only then could he turn his attention to destroying the Blue Sorcerers. *"But, I'll be there to help,'* Loche sneered. Kylasar bit back a snide reply.

"Perhaps the boy was only repeating a rumor, sir," Captain Bevel was saying. "We searched the Shadowspawn Mountains, where he said the One-Horne had been, but there was nothing there." Wondering how much pertinent information he had missed, Kylasar watched sweat slide lazily down the captain's jaw and smirked. Perhaps he should make an example of the captain.

The captain lowered his eyes. "I'll order the men to keep searching, sir."

"You do that, Captain! And, when you return, you had better have caught the One-Horne!"

"Yes, sir." The captain saluted, turned on his heel, and left the room. *Like a cur whipped soundly,* Kylasar thought. He watched the pewter cup begin to soften in the fire. He sighed, leaning back against the chair. The flames grew higher, the fire popped, and sparks arched through the air.

"Katherine is on Wry and seeks her daughter."

Impossible! Kylasar sat up. *She has no magic power, no way to get here. In fact, she has no idea that Wry exists.*

"She came through a gate at Pongeed Pool."

"What gate at Pongeed Pool? There's no gate there!"

"There is now. If you don't believe me, why don't you see for yourself?"

Kylasar rose from his chair and moved to the fireplace where a small, oval mirror on the mantle stood. He passed his hand over the glass and whispered Katherine's name. The silvery surface wavered and then cleared into a bright image of Katherine struggling to the top of a grassy embankment, where she dropped face down. *A nuisance,* he thought. She had served her purpose and given him Amanda. But now she was here to take the girl back, and he could not let that happen. Not until he had caught the One-Horne and had the Jeweled Locket in his possession. The glass clouded again.

"I'll send the Rathriders," Kylasar said.

"And if the Rathriders can't find her?"

"Then I'll magic every blade of grass, every stone, every river! The whole of Wry will be against her. She will not survive!" His mind already on the spell to call the demon-spawn Rathriders, Kylasar strode from the room.

CHAPTER FOUR

**BLESS THE 23RD AIRBORNE LIGHTER
IT HOLDS THE POWERS OF FIRE.**

Katherine turned her head to the side and felt wet hair slide across her neck. Shivering, she curled up into a fetal position to get warm and was vaguely aware of a low-timbered, melodious voice.

"She seems to be coming round."

"She was unconscious a long time." Katherine heard the second voice, not with her ears, but as if she had said the words to herself.

I must be dreaming, she thought. *I must be in bed at the motel, dreaming I followed a talking blue flame to search a strange wood for Mandy.* She snuggled into a tighter ball, crossing her arms over her chest and tucking her hands under her chin. But the cold was real. She opened her eyes. Blue-white moonlight illuminated the area in her line of vision, and she saw a dark shape bending toward her, a man.

"There! She appears to be reviving! Hello!"

Feeling dirt on her cheek, she wiped her face. *This was no dream,* she thought. She tried to respond, but her teeth were chattering and her mouth seemed frozen.

"What happened to you?" he asked.

"The water," she managed and then swallowed to clear her throat. "I tripped and fell." Then she remembered. "I think I passed out."

Again, she heard that strange voice like a projection of her own thoughts. *"You nearly drowned."* Something odd is going on, she thought. If she had fallen into the water, had she really seen the blue flame? *Where was it now?* Katherine tried to sit up, but the man's hand on her shoulder firmly pressed her back.

"Lie still a moment, and I will get a wrap to warm you," he said. In the light of the full moon, Katherine watched him fumble through a bulky leather bag. He wore a dark brown jerkin over a white collarless full-sleeved shirt open to the waist and pants tucked into thigh-high dark boots. A cord around his neck threaded through an enormous jewel that shimmered against his chest like a rainbow in the moonlight. From his bag he withdrew a piece of thin fabric, which he tucked around her body. Katherine felt the fabric generate warmth like an electric blanket. "I am Wren," he said, "guardian of Crystal Caer."

"What's a guardian?"

"A protector," Wren replied. "I guard my village."

"With my help."

Katherine jumped at the strange voice in her head. She sat up. "Did you say that?" she asked Wren.

"No," he said.

She watched his face for signs that he might be trying to trick her.

"I did."

She looked behind her and was surprised to see a large silver-haired dog resting his head on huge forepaws. His soft, amber eyes stared at her and his long bushy tail flicked lazily back and forth. He looked like the sheep dog her brother once had.

"Well, a *dog* certainly couldn't say that," she said, then turned to see the man smile.

"A dog?" Wren asked. "What is that? Shaeff is a telepack who mindspeaks, and the strange voice you hear in your head is Shaeff speaking to you. Surely there are such telepacks where you come from." The man motioned the animal toward him. Katherine shook her head and said, "Where I come from, he would be called a dog."

"Then where do you come from?" he asked.

"Akron," she said.

"Strange, I have never heard of it." He paused. "What is your name?"

"Katherine," she said. But she was wondering why he had never heard of Akron. *Everyone has heard of Akron,* Katherine thought, and she knew nonsense when she heard it. She looked at Shaeff. His mind speech was as strange as the blue flame talking to her. Shaeff yawned and stretched out on the ground next to the man. "Can Shaeff read my mind?" she asked Wren.

"I do not listen to your private thoughts unless you ask me to."

"Can you hear Shaeff when he talks to me?" Katherine asked Wren.

"I can mindspeak to you both at the same time or to just you, Katherine. For instance," the animal looked up at the man. *"Wren can be unbearable at times."* Katherine waited for Wren to reply, but Shaeff continued. *"See? That last thought I mindspoke only to you."*

"All right, Shaeff, what's going on?" Wren asked.

"I just told her that you could be unbearable." The Telepack almost seemed to smile.

"As you can see, Shaeff possesses a sense of humor," Wren said, and stood up. Katherine was still trying to digest the fact that this animal could speak to her when Wren changed the subject. "Can you walk?" he asked.

She was tired and dirty, but she felt otherwise whole. She nodded.

Smiling, Wren gently helped her to stand. With the fabric over her shoulders keeping her warm, she stood up and saw on the ground the little key she had retrieved from the rock. Planning to examine it in the morning, Katherine picked it up then shoved it into the front pocket of her wet jeans. The key clicked against her father's silver lighter, which was engraved with the words 23RD AIRBORNE. She didn't smoke, but after her father had died in her last year of high school, she had carried his lighter as a reminder of his love.

In the moonlight, the trees grew silver leaves that sparkled in the dark, the water in the pool looked like oil swirling in fluorescent colors, and rocks at the pool's edge glittered like mica. She wondered where the blue flame had gone. Again thinking she might be dreaming, she shut her eyes tight. But when she opened them, the leaves of the trees still sparkled like tinsel in the moonlight.

"That's strange!" she murmured.

Wren, arms akimbo, was now standing in front of her.

"What?"

"I don't remember this area," she answered. And, with the flame gone, she thought, she had no idea which direction to go to find Mandy. How stupid she had been to believe that a talking flame could lead her to her child. *If I can get back to my car,* she thought, *then I can start over.*

Katherine pushed her still-damp hair back from her forehead. "I must get back to my car," she said.

"What's a car?" The thought entered her mind with an inquisitive gentleness, and she looked down to see Shaeff at her side.

"A car?! It's, you know, a way of transportation." Katherine looked at Wren. "Haven't you told him about cars?" Wren looked puzzled. "Surely you know what a car is, Wren!" She watched him shake his head in the negative and suddenly, she felt fearful. *The talking blue flame, the golden key, the strange water in the pool, Shaeff's mindspeech, and now Wren's ignorance of cars.* "Come on, Wren," Katherine pleaded. "You must be joking!"

"I do not know what a car is, Katherine."

She could not seem to catch her breath. *Calm down,* she thought. "Wren, come on. I'll show you what a car is."

Wren shrugged and looked at Shaeff. Katherine turned and walked toward the trees where she thought she had entered the woods, but in the moonlight, she could not get her bearings. *And if I can't find my car, how will I ever find Mandy?* When a sharp branch cut across her cheek, she sat down on a large log. She knew now that she had never been in these woods before. She put her face into her hands and did her best to hold back the tears.

Wren took her hands into his own.

"What can we do?" His voice was low and soft.

She pulled her hands away to wipe her eyes and took a deep breath. "Please help me find my car," she said. "I have to find my car!"

"Why?"

"Without it, I can't find Mandy."

"Who is Mandy?"

"My daughter."

"Is she lost?"

Katherine felt anger constricting her chest. "Her father kidnapped her!" She tried to calm herself, then answered. "That's why I have to find my car, Wren."

Wren patted Shaeff and nodded. "Shaeff has an idea how we might help you," he said. "If you allow him to merge with your mind, all your memories will be his. Once he understands what a car is, perhaps he can help you find it. He cannot do this unless you give him permission, and once you agree, he will know you as intimately as you know yourself. You can hide nothing from him. Understand?"

Katherine looked at Shaeff. His amber eyes glowed. "It isn't possible," Katherine said.

"Then it will not hurt for you to try," Wren said.

Katherine could see his logic. That is what she had thought when she had followed the spark of blue. And what would be the harm in letting Shaeff try?

A kaleidoscope of thoughts bombarded her instantly, and some made her cheeks grow warm. But what harm could there be? She looked at Wren. Good grief, she was thinking as if she believed him! Katherine sighed, "What do I do?"

"Sit with your back against the log," Wren said. He fluffed his leather bag like a pillow and placed it behind her head. "All you do is sit back and close your eyes."

Shaeff rolled his big amber eyes up at her; she doubted he could read her mind, but she was willing to try anything to find Mandy.

"Now, Shaeff will put his head into your lap. Close your eyes," Wren commanded. Katherine did as she was told. Feeling a gentle nudge in her mind and a pressure that pulled at her wakefulness, she relaxed and felt a warmth spread through her. Following the warmth with her mind as it moved down her torso into her legs, feet, and chilled fingertips, she grew tired. And so, she fell asleep.

CHAPTER FIVE

DREAMS ARE FIGMENTS OF FANCY, THE SEEKER'S QUEST, TOO REAL.

A hooting owl woke Katherine from jumbled dreams of a laughing, two-year-old Mandy who wobbled with sagging diaper down the hall to a Christmas tree dripping with silver tinsel and of a crying Mandy with Raggedy Ann clutched tightly in hand. Katherine stretched and felt soft fur. She opened her eyes to see Shaeff asleep with his head still in her lap and Wren, smiling gently a few feet away. Her disorientation shredded like fog thinning in the heat of day. *Mandy was missing and something had happened—what? The pool!* Katherine thought that she was probably still dreaming, but the grass felt soft where she sat and smelled like sweet clover. Behind Wren, she could see trees with silver leaves sparkling in the moonlight, and when she lifted her face to look at the moon, a cool breeze blew wisps of her hair across her forehead. The owl hooted again. Her surroundings seemed too vivid for a dream. And if she were dreaming, would she feel an ache in the back of her neck? She leaned forward and pulled Wren's bag from behind her head, handed it to him, then massaged her neck. *He must have had rocks in the bag,* she thought.

"I slept so well," Katherine mumbled. She felt an inner tingling of warmth in her legs. Then she remembered why she had been asleep. The dog stirred and moved his head to his paws, eyes closed. Katherine's voice trembled, "What did Shaeff learn?"

"Shaeff learned much," Wren said, "but right now he needs to rest." From the bag that Katherine had used as a pillow, Wren took a small bundle of material that gleamed like satin in the moonlight and placed it with great care on the ground.

Katherine was convinced that Shaeff's going to sleep was a deliberate attempt at avoiding her questions. "Wren, what did Shaeff—"

"Wait!" Wren said. The warmth that Shaeff had generated through her body suddenly dissipated. Her clothes felt damp, gritty, and uncomfortable, and night was turning cold. She shivered and tried to keep her teeth from chattering. *This is ridiculous,* she thought. *I have to find my car and get into dry clothes soon, or I'll catch pneumonia.* She pulled Wren's fabric tight around her shoulders. Wren unwrapped a glittering, blue-white crystal, pushed it vertically into the soft ground, and reached back inside his bag to remove a silver U-shaped object like a two-tined dinner fork. Placing the two tines in his mouth, Wren hummed a low vibrant tone. To Katherine's amazement, when Wren pulled the silver object from his mouth, it vibrated the same pitch. With great gentleness, he placed the silver fork so that its U-shaped tines enclosed the top of the crystal and then very carefully moved the tines down until a faint blue-white light began to glow from the crystal.

Katherine stretched her hands out to the light, but she felt no heat. "It's not hot," she said. "What's it for?"

"It is a craerlyte," he said moving the silver object into his mouth and clamping it shut. The humming stopped. He tossed the silver object back into the bag. "It is for light. Why would you want light hot? You can touch it if you want."

Katherine did, and the craerlyte felt cool. Pulling her hands back, she rewrapped them in the warmth of Wren's fabric. Looking down at the strange fabric in hand, then up at the craerlyte glowing with its steady stream of blue light, she frowned. She asked aloud, "Could I dream all this?"

Wren sighed. "I will try to explain so that you can understand." He looked down at the bag on the ground. "Are you hungry?" he asked.

Katherine was shocked that she had not thought about food in a long time. "Famished!" she confessed.

"So I thought." Wren rummaged through the bag and handed her a small, dark loaf of bread. Then he removed a large green block like clay. He broke off a piece and handed it to her. She bit into the sweet tasting, nutty wheat bread, but hesitated to try the green block. "What is it?" she asked.

"Curdle."

Ugh, she thought. It had no distinctive odor, but when she took a bite, she found it tasted like mild cheddar.

Wren handed her a smooth-skinned bottle. "Go easy. You have not eaten for a while and nightroot will dull your senses if you drink too much or too fast."

She took a small sip, then, never having tasted anything so sweet and cool (like a mixture of strawberries and peaches), she guzzled it. Wren snatched the bottle away. Some of the sweet liquid spilled. She rubbed at her chin, feeling its stickiness. "I'm still thirsty!"

"I said, not too much. You are not used to its effect." Wren carefully inserted the cork in the bottle's spout.

Her mouth didn't seem to be working right. *That's odd,* she thought. Her lips were growing numb. "What did you say it is?" Katherine mumbled.

"Nightroot."

Katherine giggled.

"Nightroot?" She felt giddy, as if that one little drink had intoxicated her. Wren smiled. Within seconds, the giddiness and numbness disappeared, and she stopped laughing, feeling a little embarrassed. She felt her face flush and was thankful that in the dark Wren had not seemed to notice.

"During the mind merge," Wren said, "Shaeff found out that you are from another place called Earth."

What kind of game is he trying to play, she wondered? *Surely he is not serious.* "Of course. Where else would I be from?"

"I don't know," he said. "But you are not on Earth now. You are on Wry."

"Wry?" He must be joking, and she didn't have time for jokes. Not on Earth? The idea was too fantastic to even consider. "If—and I mean if—we are on Wry, then how did I get here? What happened to my world?"

His eyes looked through her, focused perhaps on some far away vision. "I do not know." Wren shook his head. "But Shaeff learned many things about you, and I want you to listen to a tale passed down on Wry from one generation to the next. Shaeff says it pertains to you."

I'll listen to him now, Katherine thought, *but as soon as I get through eating, I'll leave this weirdo and find my car.* Adjusting the borrowed fabric so that its warmth penetrated her damp clothes, she ate her bread and cheese while Wren recited.

"After many sun trips pass away
"On a world none can descry—
"A Seeker comes into our midst
"To find her loss on Wry.
"The Seeker finds more than her ken
"Collects the Key of K'vle,
"Travels where the Dark One rules—
"The Imperator Evil.
"A Childe of Earth, the Dark One's flesh —
"Rejects his wickedness
"Finds the magick One-Horne, then destroys her Father's quest."

The owl hooted again, and Katherine shivered and swallowed. "What does it mean?" she asked.

Wren looked carefully at Katherine. "Shaeff told me that your second name is Kylasar." He uncorked the Nightroot bottle and took a small sip.

"What does that have to do with anything?"

"The poem is about Kylasar, whom we call the Dark Imperator, an extremely dangerous sorcerer practicing in black magic."

Sorcerers and black magic? Katherine was losing all patience. "It's just coincidence, Wren."

"A prophecy says Kylasar turns against Kylasar during the Second Reign of Rhu'dammen. That time is upon us now. If the Dark Imperator is not thwarted by the Seeker, then Wry will be destroyed. Shaeff says that you, Katherine Kylasar, are the Seeker."

Wren actually seemed to believe what he was saying. His eyes never flinched from her rapt stare. It was time to leave. She stood up. "I am going to find my car."

"Sit back down, Katherine, and let me finish." The command in his voice made her hesitate.

"Finish then, so I can leave."

"You said your daughter disappeared with her father and up until the time we found you by the Pongeed Pool, you had been searching for her. True?"

"Yes, but—"

Wren waved an impatient hand to quiet her. *"The Seeker comes into our midst, to find her loss on Wry,* Katherine. You have the Seeker's name, and you are searching for an *Earth Childe.* Is this not you?"

Katherine struggled to keep her sense of reality. If Wren was not joking with her, how could she account for what he said? Yes, she was looking for her daughter and yes, her last name was Kylasar, but she was not on some strange world called Wry. She had followed a spark of blue into a wooded area somewhere between Akron and Pittsburgh. The idea that she was dreaming seemed the only logical conclusion. "It's merely coincidence, Wren. That's all."

"Did you not find the Key of K'vle?" he asked.

"The key?" Even as she spoke, Katherine remembered the little golden key in her pocket. If it was the same key that Wren asked about, if she had found the Key of K'vle, would that mean that Wren was right? And that she was on Wry and not dreaming? She pulled the key from her pocket and handed it to Wren. "I found it in the rocks at the edge of the pool. Is it the Key of K'vle? You tell me."

She was aware that she sounded much too defensive.

Then Shaeff, his eyes pinpoints of amber flame, stood regarding her. *"Now that I am awake, let us leave for Crystal Caer."*

Wren handed the key back to Katherine, then pulled the craerlyte from the ground. Katherine's mood darkened as she stuffed the key back into her pocket. *No one will boss me around,* she thought, *least of all a dog.* "If you think I'm going anywhere with you two, you are mistaken! I have to get back to my car."

Wren paused in putting the craerlyte into the bag. He looked up at her and shook his head. "It is not on Wry, Katherine. Where else can you look?"

His words stung, but Katherine had not found her car. Her defiance melted away, leaving her feeling like a little girl who had been scolded by adults. If she were dreaming, would it hurt to go with them? Probably not, but if she weren't dreaming and this were real, then she would be on her own in the dark, in a strange place, lost without food and water. Her decision made, she sighed and stood up. "I'm coming."

CHAPTER SIX

THE POWERS OF WATER RESIDE WITHIN THE SACRED BAND.

Trudging through the dark forest, Katherine wished she were back in the car on her way to the motel. She had tried talking to Shaeff, but he had disappeared into the dark. When she asked Wren why they were going to Crystal Caer, he merely ignored her. So they walked in silence between tall, dark trees with moonlight trickling down the straight trunks and splashing silver puddles across the ground in front of her.

Once her eyes grew accustomed to the dark, Katherine noticed faint yellow and green dots blinking from deep within bushes, a thick darkness under the trees. She wondered if animals watched from the dark bushes and tried to stay close to Wren, but she had to walk fast, and she was getting tired. Katherine's ragged breathing sounded loud to her ears. The owl no longer hooted, but crickets and tree frogs chirped noisily, and when a nearby bullfrog croaked, Katherine jumped.

She watched Wren walk in front of her with the long easy stride of an experienced hiker. *I didn't know I'd need hiking boots,* she thought miserably. The bottoms of her feet hurt from stepping on occasional stones, and her legs ached from walking for hours on springy moss that pulled at the back of her calves with each step. Resentment flared in Katherine and at a tree with thick roots poking from the ground, she stopped to catch her breath.

"Wren!" she called. "Can't we rest?"

He turned toward her, not even breathing hard. In the moonlight, she saw his mouth curve into a broad smile above the sparkle of the jewel on his chest. "I had wondered how long it would take you to yield your stubbornness," he said. He dropped his bag, motioned for her to sit, and then whistled shrilly.

Shaeff rambled out of the darkness, his tongue hanging from his mouth. *"You whistled?"* He panted.

Katherine wondered why Shaeff was allowing her to eavesdrop and then thought that if this were her dream and she wanted to hear him, she would.

"Yes," Wren said. He nodded at Katherine. "She needs rest."

"I am going to scout around." And Shaeff disappeared into the sable night.

Katherine sat against a tree and leaned her head back against rough bark and closed her eyes. "My feet hurt," she said.

She felt a tug on her boot and opened her eyes. Before she could stop him, Wren had slipped her boot off. Not yet trusting him, she cautiously watched him bend the leather uppers. Wren removed the second boot and sat on the mossy ground.

"These boots are as stiff as that tree you sit against," he said.

"I'll never get them back on," she said.

"I cannot help your feet right now," he said, "but how about your stomach. Are you hungry?"

"No, but could I please have some Nightroot?"

Wren smiled. He rummaged through his bag for the bottle and handed it to her. In spite of everything, he was trying to be nice. When he remarked casually, "Not too much," Katherine quickly changed her mind about his affability. She took a deliberately large gulp and handed the bottle back.

"There's your precious Nightroot," she said and, wanting more to drink, glared at him. Instead of asking for more, she stuffed her hands into her pants' pockets and touched the cool, smooth planes of her father's lighter. She rubbed her thumb across the inscription as if the lighter were a worry stone. Maybe now Wren would answer her questions. "When will we get to Crystal Caer?" she asked.

He leaned back on his hands and looked up into the inky darkness. "We should be there by sun-strike."

"What is sun-strike?"

"When the sun strikes the horizon," he answered. *He must mean sunrise,* she thought. "And why are we going there?"

"To talk to a friend of mine. Maybe he can convince you that you are the Seeker."

Katherine smiled. So Wren did not think she had fallen hook, line, and sinker for his tale. She pulled her hands from her pockets, her right hand holding her father's lighter. Wanting to see Wren's expression, to see whether he was putting her on or not, she flicked the lighter. The yellow-red flame flickered then cast orange light across Wren's face, and on it, she saw a look of terror. Wren scuttled backward into thick brush.

"Wren!" she called. "What's wrong?" What had he seen? She jumped to her feet and immediately, the sound of a hundred wind chimes tinkled through the night and, like a flock of curious birds swooping crazily from the silver-leaved treetops, flickering blue-white flames descended to touch her hands, brush against her face, and cover her from head to toe. As they danced and twirled and fluttered across her tingling skin, she was awestruck but unafraid. The flames spun closer in an intricate dance until she was embraced by blue fire, and soft musical notes brushed feather-like melodies into a symphony of insistence forcing her forward. Startled, she realized that she was floating through the forest. Still, Katherine felt no fear, only elation and wonder. She closed her eyes to concentrate on the music, expecting to hear the voice of the blue spark that had brought her through the woods.

The symphony dissolved into a series of simple notes that led her thoughts down a spiraling mental path. She moved through her mind, traveling ever deeper until she felt heat so intense, so purposeful that she wanted to stop. Still the notes, a siren's song, pulled her forward. She entered a part of her mind she had never visited before, a new room where mental power fired her anguish in missing Mandy into a passion with purpose and determination. Intuitively, she understood this power could find her daughter, if she only knew how to use it.

Katherine opened her eyes. Still cloaked in the blue flames, she stood before a clear crystal cairn a foot away. Imbedded in the uppermost section of crystal was a circlet sparkling like a crown of intricately braided, silver laser filaments. The circlet rose through the crystal to hover above the cairn. Two blue flames detached themselves from her arm and when they touched the circlet became two blue gems. The silver blue-gemmed circlet floated toward her and, as it descended to rest on her head, she heard the notes in her mind crescendo and blinding blue lightning struck the center of the cairn.

"Katherine!"

She gasped. The voice was that of the blue flame! She lifted her flame covered arms to look for the blue flame that had spoken, but another lightning bolt crashed against the cairn.

"Know you that your daughter dear
flees from the Dark One's lands—
And while upon this world called Wry
Her fate is in your hands."

When her vision cleared, Katherine saw that the cairn had disappeared. A tinkling sound as if from a fairy harpsichord echoed and then faded from her mind. Tinkling like wind chimes, the blue flames darted from her body and then vanished into the dark forest. The circlet thrummed against her temples. She thought her eyes had deceived her, but the band felt real when she touched it.

When a twig snapped behind her, Katherine turned, alert, lethargy gone. Wren, her boots in hand, was edging toward her into filtered starlight. Katherine sensed his exhaustion and something else. Agitation or frustration?

His eyes were fixed upon the circlet around her forehead. "The Band of Brocoudahl!" he exclaimed, and he fell to his knees, head to the ground.

"Get up!" she cried. Why was he groveling at her feet? Had he lost his senses? "What are you talking about?"

"You were holding the flame!" He stood up. "That is blasphemy for all but the Seeker! Were you not burnt?"

He reached for her hands. Remembering the blue lightning and afraid it might strike him down, Katherine jerked back, stepping quickly away from his touch. The thrumming stopped, and suddenly, all the excitement soured her stomach.

"No, I wasn't burnt. I merely flicked my father's lighter! See?"

She pulled the lighter from her pocket and demonstrated. Wren stepped back with his arms covering his head. He seemed terrified of the flame. "You must be the Seeker!" he said lowering his arms. "To hold the flame is blasphemy for all but the Seeker."

Shaeff trotted to Wren's side. *"The Band of Brocoudahl is just the beginning."*

"None of this makes any sense!" Katherine was growing more confused. "What does it mean to be the Seeker?"

"It means that if you are the Seeker, you can draw upon the Powers of Fire, Earth, Water, and Air. You will need those powers to find your daughter."

Katherine remembered the words of the blue flame. *"Her fate is in your hands,"* and fear rose in her chest. If finding Mandy depended on her using Powers of Fire, Earth, Water, and Air, then she would fail. "How do I draw upon the Powers, Wren? I don't know how!"

"That's why we go to Crystal Caer. My friend there will know how."

Katherine thought that her life was becoming a nightmare. As she put the lighter away, she noticed that she stood in her stocking feet. "My boots!"

Sheepishly, Wren picked them up. "You had better put these back on."

While putting her boots on, Katherine felt the cold metal of the silver circlet above her eyebrows. She was not dreaming. There were too many little details that her own imagination could have never have made up. Katherine now knew she was on Wry, because Mandy was here. The blue flame had convinced her.

She noticed Shaeff's large amber eyes on her. *"I would not get too attached to the powers. They can destroy you, if not used properly."* Then Shaeff turned and disappeared into the forest.

CHAPTER SEVEN

BLESSED BE THE POWERS OF SPIRIT FOR THE SEEKER'S POWER GROWS.

As the night softened into a predawn flush, Katherine's thoughts grew more confused. She had passed her physical limits hours before, and the memory of the blue flames leading her to the Band of Brocoudahl was fading, but she kept trying to make some sense of the power she had felt in the light in her mind. *Is that where magic comes from?* she wondered. Could she use magic to find Mandy? It did not seem possible. She thought about the blue flame. Should she tell Wren and Shaeff about it? If what the flame had said was true, then Mandy was here. And here was Wry, not Earth. What about Eric? Would he be here, too? She thought about the poem that Wren had recited. Could Eric be . . . what was it? A Dark Imperator? She remembered one time when Eric had offered an old watchman a cup of rusty water, insisting that it was beef broth. She had thought it an evil thing to do, but Eric had called it a joke. If she had known Eric was evil, she would never have married him. Katherine tried to puzzle it out. Nothing made sense.

Now Wren, on a hillock ahead of her, stood looking out over a large valley of tall yellow grass spreading northward. She stopped beside him.

Purple-black mountains blocked the early morning rays of sun and rose precariously high on the valley's eastern slope. Wren handed her the Nightroot. She took a sip and passed the bottle back. He drank. Nodding toward the valley, he said, "Crystal Caer is there. We should be there by the time the sun shines over the mountains."

He pointed toward a hill curving against the sky before them. On the side of the hill, etched in white chalk, she saw a huge stick figure of a man standing inside a rectangle. Around the man's head were lines like spokes from a wagon wheel. Or, Katherine thought, like the rays of the sun. "What is it?" she asked.

"Belanos," Wren replied. "Our god, who resides in the sun."

"Why is his picture on the hillside?"

"To protect Crystal Caer."

Katherine could hear pride in his voice, and she turned to the hillside to look for the village. She saw nothing but the hillside, not even smoke curling into the sky. "Where is the village?"

"Crystal Caer sits inside the hill."

"So, how do we get inside?"

Wren laughed. "We go through the gate!" He began moving down a gently sloping incline with Shaeff, already far ahead. Gnats and other small insects zipped around Katherine's feet while bees darted through the tall stalks slick with morning dew. From Wren's careless passage, the thick yellow stalks whipped back and forth, and when a stalk flipped her eye, Katherine opened her mouth to scream at him. Wren chose that moment to halt, and she bumped full-bodied into him.

"Oaf!" she sputtered, stumbling backward.

"What?" He turned around. The jewel on his chest sparkled in the morning sun.

Embarrassed, her face flushed. She was tired of walking and felt as if Wren were taking her on a wild goose chase. "Can't you give me a warning or something that you're stopping?"

"You should pay more attention to where you are going, Katherine, instead of walking with your head in the clouds." Evidently he was refusing to let her antagonize him. He smiled and turned to point past the tassels of grass. "Look there," he said.

A shiny wall, sparkling like mica with flecks of silver in the morning sun, extended above the crest of the hill. Shaeff was waiting for them in front of an arched opening like a black hole that absorbed all external light. Wren scrambled up the slope and disappeared through the archway. Shaeff trotted in after him. Once Katherine stood under the archway she paused in claustrophobic dread, her knees shaking. She hated the dark! And the smell of rancid air added to the feeling that she was being sucked into a black void. Sweat dripped down her cheeks, and her mouth felt dry. Blinking her eyes, waiting for them to adjust to the dark, Katherine gasped when a hand took hers.

"It is just me," Wren said.

He squeezed her hand, and she lost her fear as he gently pulled her into the darkness. This was Wren's home, she realized, and he had passed this way a hundred times. He led without any hesitation, and when he stopped, Katherine bumped into his back, again.

"I wish you'd stop doing that!" she hissed.

"Sorry," Wren said.

The dark seemed to press against her, and she tried to take slow breaths. One night when she was four, she had been chasing fireflies and crawled under the front porch and gotten stuck on a nail. By the time her mother had found her, she had been stung all over her body by fire ants. Now, biting her lip, she tried not to think about things that could sneak up and sting her in the dark.

A brilliant flash startled her, and she tasted blood. Pink light filled the air. She blinked and noticed that the crystal on the thong around Wren's neck was glowing like a pink neon light. Now she could see that she stood between walls of black basalt in a short hallway with two massive, metallic doors opposite the archway. When Wren, with Shaeff at his heels, picked up the crystal still attached to the thong around his neck and moved it closer to the doors, Katherine saw a round indentation shoulder high on the right door. Wren placed the crystal into the roundness, and the pink light was utterly extinguished. The massive doors swung inward into bright morning sunlight.

Blinded again, Katherine stumbled through the doors, blinked, and felt a whoosh when the massive doors shut swiftly behind her. When her eyes focused, her attention riveted on Crystal Caer, three terraces before her in a circular pit. A road ran from the metal doors down an incline and over the terraces, like giant stair steps, toward the center of the village. Small trees, some bearing a bright blue fruit, were set in giant planters along the road. Round houses with thatched roofs and walls of chalk sat along walkways circling back to meet the road, like a radius through Crystal Caer. The door frame of a house on the highest terrace to Katherine's left was painted in bright colors and strange patterns, while beyond that house, another door frame, like a totem pole, was shaped into bulging human and animal faces. Between all the houses, Katherine saw gardens filled with yellow, pink, red, and purple flowering bushes spilling over shiny black rock courtyards. Along the walkway at the edge of the terrace, a retaining wall was covered with trailing ivy that hung down to the lower terrace, some fifteen feet below.

A white-haired bearded man in a belted, long tunic stepped from a house on her right and strode toward Wren. "Wren," he called. "Welcome home!" The man clasped Wren around the shoulders.

Katherine watched the village come to life. An elderly woman moved from her doorway to the black retaining wall and called down to someone on the lower terrace. Within minutes, the early morning was filled with cacophonies of bass and soprano voices raised in greeting Wren. A woman with long blonde tresses, delicate features, and green slanted eyes ran up the road to Wren and embraced him tightly. He kept his arm around her while he conversed with the man with the white beard. Katherine felt Shaeff's hot, moist breath on the back of her leg through her denim jeans, and feeling conspicuous, she watched the villagers patting Wren on the back, asking him about things and places that Katherine knew nothing about. She crossed her arms.

Some men wore multicolored short tunics with baggy trousers underneath and many wore cloaks similar to the one that Wren had lent her still hanging over her shoulders. The women wore a longer version of the tunic. Some men and women wore leather boots, although most were barefoot. Past the circle of villagers and the woman (who was not moving from Wren's side), a tall man, with dark hair curled past his shoulders who wore a black robe like a monk's habit, pushed his way through the crowd. A short-cropped beard hugged his square jaw, and a mustache outlined his finely sculpted mouth. The man stopped directly in front of Katherine. "Oh, ho! Wren! What have we here?"

Most people moved back, and all eyes turned from Wren to Katherine. *Everyone is staring at me,* she thought, and she felt herself blushing. The woman at Wren's side moved behind him, but Wren and the white-headed man stood their ground.

Katherine squirmed under the hardening ice-blue eyes. *Whoever he is,* she thought stubbornly, *he will not tell me what to do.* She raised her chin in defiance and watched a slow, puzzled frown form on his face.

"Serhonydd,—" Wren said.

"Silence, Wren!" Serhonydd interrupted, raising a finger to his lips.

Katherine was embarrassed for Wren. "His manners need improving, don't they?" she asked Wren. Serhonydd's eyes darkened like deep well water. She offered him her hand. "Nice to meet you, Sir. I'm—"

"Enough!" Serhonydd's voice boomed like thunder. His eyes were now as dark as midnight clouds. "I know who you are!" he whispered.

Shocked by his tone and lack of manners, Katherine stepped back and tripped over Shaeff. Serhonydd grabbed her by the arm and pulled her close to his chest before she could regain her balance. He whispered against her ear, "Do not say anything, please!" and he set her back on her feet. She felt her face flush and ignored the stares and laughter from the crowd as she brushed herself free of his strong hands.

"Follow me!" he demanded. *I'll follow you,* Katherine thought rebelliously, *but only because I want to.* She moved down the road behind the flowing thick robes of the dark-haired man and decided that it might be a very interesting morning.

CHAPTER EIGHT

THE REALM OF NORM TWISTS INTO ODD, AND WHAT WAS KNOWN IS GONE.

The crowd parted before them, and Serhonydd led Katherine down the incline flanked by houses. With expressions of wonder and fear, people watched from doorways. Should she trust Serhonydd? He said he knew who she was. Had Shaeff forewarned him about her being the Seeker? And why didn't Serhonydd want the villagers to know who she was? He did not act very friendly, and he seemed arrogant, yet calm and self-assured. But if he could help her find Mandy, she would happily put up with his arrogance. She decided she would do whatever Wren thought she should do.

At an open doorway of a windowless large house with sand-colored walls, Serhonydd stopped and turned to the crowd, then waited like an actor on stage until all eyes were on him. "Everybody, about your own business!" he said. Then with a long-fingered hand, he waved the villagers away.

Serhonydd stood aside, and Wren and Shaeff stepped over the threshold and disappeared. Serhonydd motioned for Katherine to enter the darkness. She stared at him thinking, *does he think I will blindly obey?* Then, exasperated by his silence, she walked quickly past him, over the threshold into darkness.

Before her, a blue light spilled from a doorway, over the floor and across a length of short hall. Moving forward through this second door, Katherine entered a windowless circular room bright with blue light radiating from craerlytes set like torches on the walls. After her eyes adjusted, she noticed a smooth stone floor strewn with plump cushions sloping toward a three-foot-high stone wall that surrounded a shallow pit. In the center of the pit, a round red-orange crystal glowed like fire. Its light and the blue light from craerlytes reflected and cast an eerie glow from strange swords and shields hanging around the room. Shaeff moved into the pit and stretched out, his head on his paws.

"Sit down," Serhonydd said. Wren dropped onto a cushion, and Katherine slumped on a pillow beside him.

"Do you feel all right?" Wren asked.

She didn't feel all right, and she never would feel all right until she had found Mandy. "I guess I'm tired and hungry," she said. She tried to blink the tears away.

"And depressed?"

Turning toward Shaeff, she thought, *You know how I feel?*

"I know your mind was troubled when I touched it. Things are no better now, yes?"

Katherine wiped her eyes.

No better, she thought, *only more confusing.*

"Serhonydd will help you."

Serhonydd was now standing over her, holding a goblet in each hand. She took a goblet and sipped. *Warm grape juice,* she thought, *but good.* Serhonydd handed the second goblet to Wren and then motioned to the back of the room.

A small man, his face full of deep wrinkles, stepped from the darkness and smiled gently at her. On the top of the wall around the pit, he carefully set a tray laden with yellow and brown pots. A delicious aroma filled the air. The man left the room, and Serhonydd handed her a wooden spoon from the tray and a yellow pot of what smelled like the vegetable soup she cooked on winter days. The white lumps tasted a lot like chicken, and the green vegetable was cabbage. The pleasure of filling her empty stomach made her smile.

"All right?" Serhonydd asked.

"Delicious!" she mumbled, her mouth full.

"It is the first hot meal she has eaten since we found her," Wren said, his eyes on his bowl.

"Well then, let her eat." Serhonydd. His startlingly deep blue eyes watched Katherine's face.

Uncomfortable with his intense inspection, Katherine blushed and pretended to concentrate on her food. When she chanced to look up at him again, Serhonydd had returned to his food.

After eating, Katherine, full and feeling drowsy, wanted nothing more than a soft fluffy bed to curl up in, but Serhonydd stepped over the wall into the pit and Shaeff sat up and tipped his head back to hold what seemed to Katherine like a private conversation with Serhonydd. She grew uncomfortable thinking that they were talking about her. Why else would they not be talking aloud? Then Serhonydd returned to stand in front of her. "Katherine," he said, "you must be brave. For your daughter's sake!"

She did not feel brave. She felt confused and lost in a strange place where nothing was normal. *Maybe Alice had felt the same in Wonderland,* she thought. She remembered reading the book to Mandy. She might never read to her daughter again.

Shaeff was easing himself against her, and Katherine wrapped her arms around him and cried. Her pain was Shaeff's pain, and the dog seemed to shake as if he shared her misery. After wiping her wet cheeks with the palm of her hand, Katherine hugged him until they both calmed down.

"Well," Serhonydd said smiling, "now that you have that over with, maybe we can go on. Eh?"

Wren exhaled a long breath, and Shaeff briskly shook himself and then put his soft head on her lap.

Serhonydd looked askance at Katherine. "From what Shaeff tells me," he said, "you are from Earth."

"That sums it up fairly well," Katherine muttered, thinking how ludicrous it sounded. "Aren't we all?"

Serhonydd shook his head. "Wren and I are not. Only you are, Katherine."

"Wren told me that, but I don't believe either of you." Katherine felt a surge of anger mingled with fear. *If they are trying to scare me,* she thought, *then they are doing a good job of it.*

Serhonydd quietly regarded Katherine. "Legends say Earth is a country far east of Crystal Caer on another continent. Although no one knows where Earth is, I know from written histories that the Dru'dammen came from its Isle of Anglesby to the land of Wry. Wren's ancestors, the Yttoshamen, have always lived in Wry but my ancestors, the Dru'dammen came from Earth. Like you, Katherine." He paused for a sip from his goblet. "Since you are from Earth, where is the Isle of Anglesby?" Serhonydd asked in a quiet voice.

Maybe it was a mistake to come here, she thought. *Maybe if I had stayed near the pond, my life would have returned to normal. Maybe my subconscious mind created an illusion called Wry, but then again, everything around me seems real.* "How would I know?"

Serhonydd said. "The histories say the Dru'dammen were once Druids persecuted by the Roman, Plautius, during the reign of Tiberius Caesar."

"I've heard about the Druids," Katherine interrupted. "But they vanished soon after a battle between the Celtic Queen Boudica and the Romans."

"That's because the Arch-Druid, Horab, summoned the *Dryacraeft* to ask the revealer of secrets, the *ys yw wedydd*, to find a gate to a new land. Now, watch." Serhonydd waved his hand toward the center of the pit, where a dark cloud spread a three-dimensional screen above the dimming faerlyte. Within the cloud, images began to form of a clearing in dark viridian pine trees, where stood a circle of men in long black hooded robes. One man silently separated himself from the circle and moved beside a lone figure in the middle.

"Horab," the second man said and took from beneath his black robe a stone the size of a walnut wrapped in gold wire hanging from a gold serpentine chain. "If we cast the *Anguinvm*, the adder stone, to find the gate to a new land, it may be destroyed."

"It is the only chance we have, *Ys Yw Wedydd*," Horab replied. "If we do not want our people to die, we must escape to a new land."

The *ys yw wedydd* bowed his head. "So be it, Horab," he said. The two men moved back to join the circle of men. The *ys yw wedydd* removed the stone from its gold wire to balance it on his upturned palm. His eyes closed and he chanted, "Belanos, son of Lord Dagda and Lady Brighid, hear our plea, guide our magic, find a gate between the worlds, deliver us from our enemies!"

The *ys yw wedydd* tossed the stone into the center of the circle and a bolt of blue lightning crackled *up* from the stone. Then the ground in the center of the circle was alive with squirming, hissing, electric blue vipers that melded into a cobalt blue mass. From the mass a viper, its eyes like black mica, rose straight up into the air. Another followed, curling along the body of the first and froze, to be followed by another and another, until over the adder stone the blue vipers arched, forming a frame like an open doorway.

As soon as the gate was complete, the *ys yw wedydd* stepped into the circle and picked up the adder stone. "Thanks be to Belanos," he intoned, then rubbed the stone over each viper, whose scaled skin hardened into delicate ice. Then with a crackle, blue lightning zipped from the vipers to close the gate with a film of blue. With a sound like a tearing sheet, the blue film split open. Through the gate, where once only the circle of men could be seen, a blue-lit path ran between silver-leaved trees. Handing the adder stone to Horab, the *ys yw wedydd* said: "The gate will last until all have fled to the new land. Guard the *Anguinvm* well, Horab. Once on the other side, you must fling it through the gate to destroy the link. Otherwise, our enemies will follow."

The image of the circle of men and the gate grew blurry at its outermost edge and, as Katherine watched, faded back into the dark smokescreen, which disappeared. Katherine turned to Serhonydd. "Did that really happen?" she asked.

"Yes."

"But all that seems like magic."

Serhonydd sighed.

"The Druids used magic to find Wry, and still today, most Dru'dammen are magically adept."

"But there is no magic on Earth, Serhonydd," Katherine said patiently.

"During the reign of my ancestors there was. But they brought it with them to Wry."

"If it takes magic to get from Earth to Wry, Serhonydd, then how did I get here?"

Serhonydd frowned.

"I don't know, Katherine. Once, I read that Earth and Wry existed as two separate worlds joined by paths called twisted planes. Here, let me show you."

He removed his belt and put its ends together to form a circular loop, flat on both sides. "With the ends joined so, there are two separate sides, one inside and one outside the belt. See?"

Katherine nodded.

"Someone standing on the inside of the belt could circumscribe the belt and never touch the outside. Someone walking on the outside would never touch the inside. Now, watch." Serhonydd dropped the ends with a flourish, twisted the belt in the middle, then put the ends back together again. "Now, Katherine, put your finger on one side of the belt and move it around until it comes back to the same place."

Katherine leaned forward, placed her finger on the outside plane of the belt and moved her finger to the twist. Her finger was now touching the inside of the belt, but she had not moved her finger from the original plane. "When I get to the twist," she said, "my finger moves from the outside to the inside of the belt, but I am on the same surface from where I started!"

"Exactly! And like the belt, twisted planes somehow connect the two worlds, Earth and Wry." Serhonydd retied his belt. "The *ys yw wedydd* used the archway to make a twist in space, and when they walked from the plane of Earth, they arrived on the plane of Wry. Then Horab broke the connection with the adder stone, and the twisted plane was lost."

Serhonydd leaned forward, his blue eyes bright with reflected concentration. "Horab and his followers discovered people much like themselves, the Yttoshamen, who lived in what they called the land of Wry. These Yttoshamen fought strange creatures, evil brigands, ogres, shapeshifters, and Rathriders sent by a sorcerer who lived northwest of Crystal Caer, past Shadowspawn Mountains in a high island fortress called the Keep. The Keep, which belongs to the sorcerer, Kylasar. I think Shaeff used the term 'ex-husband' for Kylasar's relationship to you."

Katherine felt her cheeks grow warm with anger. "Eric Kylasar, my ex-husband, is not a sorcerer."

"I feel your disbelief, Katherine, but it is true. Kylasar is the Dark Imperator. No one knows his origins or age, but he was alive and working in darkness when Horab settled Wry's Ken over a thousand years ago."

How could she sit here and listen to this? "If that's true," Katherine said with more conviction than she felt, "then my Eric is not your Kylasar, because Eric was only twenty when we married."

"Perhaps he only looked twenty, Katherine, but the Yttoshamen have tales about Kylasar that go back to the conception of Wry itself."

Wren nodded. "We believe," Wren said, "that Kylasar is the son of Loche, the God of Chaos."

Eric had been nothing more than a twenty-year-old college student, she thought, *trying to get through finals, trying to grow up and make a home for himself and his family.* She felt as if what she had thought of as reality was being twisted and flipped inside out. "Eric was an orphan. His parents died shortly after he was born." Katherine spoke as if she were yelling into gale forces.

"Katherine." Serhonydd's voice was low and patient. "Kylasar is a magician, sorcerer, 'thing' if you will, that feeds on destruction and chaos. What form of being he truly is, only he himself can say."

Katherine hated Eric for all the times he had hurt her, the times he had pulled her hair in the car, the times he had twisted her arm, and the times he had hit her. That's why she had divorced him when Mandy was five. Katherine had not wanted Mandy to grow up seeing her mother abused by her father. But he was not a sorcerer! "If Eric and Kylasar are one and the same," she said, "and I'm not saying I believe them to be the same person, but if they are, then why would Eric have brought Mandy to Wry?"

"I do not understand why he brought your daughter here," Serhonydd said. "But I do know the god and goddess have chosen you, Katherine."

Katherine said sarcastically, "Chosen me? For what?"

"To fulfill the prophecy: The Seeker will come to Wry to retrieve that which she lost."

"But how can you believe that I am the Seeker?"

Serhonydd smiled. "You wear Lord Dagda's and Lady Brighid's crown upon your head."

"The Band of Brocoudahl?" She had forgotten the silver band that she wore and reached up to touch it with her fingers. "Who are Lord Dagda and Lady Brighid?"

"They are our heavenly parents, Katherine," Wren replied in an awed voice. "The god and goddess who created all."

Serhonydd waved Wren into silence. "You are the Seeker that Yttoshamen chronicles have foretold comes to Wry. And the magical Band of Brocoudahl is just the first tool given you by Lord Dagda and Lady Brighid to help thwart Kylasar and get your daughter back. You will need many things to help you in your search for your daughter."

Katherine had seen no evidence that the band around her head was magical. But no matter what Serhonydd said, she was still here. She could see and hear Serhonydd, feel Shaeff's soft fur and his warmth, and taste and smell the soup and grape drink. Until she woke up in bed in the motel, she had to believe this world existed. For Mandy's sake, if nothing else. "I will not leave Wry," Katherine said, "until I get my daughter back."

"Good," Serhonydd said, "but you must remember Kylasar is a powerful adversary with magic greater than that of most Dru'dammen Blue Sorcerers. Kylasar's slave masters, the Rathriders with their demon Bat-mounts, enslaved the Yttoshamen to build his Keep and Keepsburg. Thousands of Yttoshamen were maimed and killed near Keepsburg. Kylasar moved east, trying to enslave the Dru'dammen at Wry's Ken and the Yttoshamen at Crystal Caer, but over the centuries, the Blue Sorcerers weakened his hold in the east. Only by small miracles have we kept him at bay. Ten years ago, the Blue Sorcerers felt changes across Wry in the energy channels where magic flows. Rathriders, shape-shifters, brigands, and demons disappeared across Wry. Then Kylasar disappeared. Some thought he had destroyed himself. With Kylasar gone, his sycophant priests grew lax and no longer ruled Keepsburg with an iron thumb. Their church had no magical power to enforce the rules. Once the citizens of Keepsburg realized that, they fought to survive as freemen. Then ten sun-strikes ago, Kylasar returned. Now his furnaces at the Keep burn day and night to rebuild his power. The maiming and killing begins again."

Serhonydd paused for breath, then continued. "I spent the last ten years at a hermitage seeking the True Path, a way of nonviolence and enlightenment. I never imagined that Kylasar and his evil would return to Wry. Now I must talk to the *ys yw wedydd's* descendants, the

Blue Sorcerers at Wry's Ken. With Kylasar's return and your appearance, we should waste no time, Katherine." Serhonydd looked at her. "The prophecies are true."

The tale Serhonydd told was hard to believe. Yet, she mused, in being so strange, how could it be other than truth? "I believe what you tell me about this sorcerer, but I won't believe your Kylasar is my Eric until I see him with my own eyes."

"You will go to Wry's Ken then?" Serhonydd asked.

"Will I learn where to find my daughter and how to return with her to Earth?"

"We can only hope," Serhonydd said.

"Can Wren and Shaeff go with me?"

Serhonydd nodded, "If they want."

Katherine could tell from Wren's expression that he was eager to go with her. She sighed. "Then I will go to Wry's Ken."

Wren stood and helped Katherine to her feet. To Wren Serhonydd said, "We must prepare for the journey. I want to leave tonight."

"If I may speak?" Wren asked.

"What?"

"Katherine needs another pair of boots."

Serhonydd looked down at her feet and laughed. "Ah, I see what you mean, Wren." He looked at Katherine. What she saw in Serhonydd's dark blue eyes she could not fathom, but somehow she knew that this man would become very important to her.

CHAPTER NINE

UPON THE STROKE OF MIDBLACK BELLS THE CHILDE SLIPS FROM HER CELL.

Mandy leaned her forehead against two wrought-iron rails and looked over the balcony. Far below, she could see rocks and a churning sea. Moonlight bounced like liquid mercury along the incoming waves, but a chill wind blew in from the sea and whipped her long hair against her shoulders. She licked salt from her lips. Although the balcony was uncomfortable, she thought it the best place to be in her tower prison. If she lifted her gaze and looked straight out to the horizon, she could see only water. But if she tipped her head back and looked up, she could see white flashes around the roof of her tower prison. *Birds,* she thought. If she watched them too long, they made her feel dizzy. She wished she too could fly high above the tower prison, into the spray of sea. She wished she were free, and she hated her father for locking her up.

When she had first seen the Keep, she had been excited. It had looked like a castle from King Arthur's days, and she had wanted to explore its every nook and cranny. But her father had locked her away. "For your own safety," he had said. That had been over a week ago, and she still did not understand him.

She wished her father was like other fathers, ones who laughed with their children, who took their children to the park, who hugged their children and tucked them into bed at night. But he had never been like that. He had always been very strict, and she had had to mind her manners and obey his every command. But now she was angry with him, and she felt rebellious. Why should she have to obey him and stay in this tower?

Mandy remembered when her father had told her mother that they would be going to Pittsburgh for the weekend. Then her father had driven them to a boarded up shack that led down into the bowels of the earth. Mandy shuddered, remembering the musty air like old unwashed laundry. She had stepped carefully onto the first stone step and followed her father down slippery steps, twisting down and around. The light in her father's hand had barely illuminated wet gray stone walls where she walked behind him. She was just beginning to wonder if the steps would go on forever, when they had come to a narrow passageway, the ceiling dripping with water. Afraid she would slip on the wet stone floor, she ran her hand along the wall for support. A many legged bug skittered across the tips of her fingers. Shrieking, she slapped at her clothes to make sure it was not crawling on her. The light flickered over her.

"What is wrong, Amanda?"

"Bugs," she whispered and then she saw light coming from an opening just beyond her father. At the end of the passageway she stopped, her eyes blinking from the glare of bright blue sky and then stepped from the stone-floored granite enclosure onto soft, velvety green grass at the top of a hill. Curving around the bottom of the hill and angling to her left, a road led toward a purple mountain rising into the sky.

When she had asked her father how they had ended up on top of a hill after traveling down into the ground, he had shrugged and said, "I don't know. Maybe a space warp or magic." Mandy had wanted to laugh, but she dared not. Then a shrill whistle had pierced the air. Turning, she saw a large black horse gallop over the top of the hill and stop beside her father.

In the saddle in front of her father, Mandy had seemed to fly down the hill along the road toward the horizon. Up a winding trail into the mountain, she spied a small village, but at once, her attention was drawn beyond the village to a gray stone fairy-tale castle that perched on the top of the mountain. Four tall turrets rose into a blue and vermilion sky, where the setting sun flashed crimson. Mandy thought it odd that the top of the turrets were capped with plain black metal roofs that looked like candle-snuffers. One lone blood-red pendant flapped in the wind.

"There is the Keep, Amanda," her father had said. "That is where we are going."

It might have looked like a fairy-tale castle then, but with nothing to do and no television, she had soon grown bored. Oh, in her tower prison there were a few dusty books about animal husbandry, whatever that meant, but there was nothing good to read, no stories like those she had loved back home.

Mandy sighed heavily. Desperate to talk to someone, she turned and stepped from the balcony back into the room. For the hundredth time, she took inventory. On her right was a small feather bed and at its foot, a paneled screen hid the toilet and wash basin. On her left sat a round, wooden table with two squat chairs on either side and a shelf built into the stone wall behind it. Across from the balcony door stood the massive, locked wooden door that led from the tower room into the Keep.

A loud rapping sounded at the door.

"Lady Amanda, your supper's here."

Mandy listened impatiently as the bolt slid back.

"Lady Amanda?" The door swung inward and hazel eyes peeked at Mandy from a girl's small face, outlined with short reddish hair. Looking thin, underfed, almost anorexic in a gauze shift with a long leather tunic tied around her middle, the girl struggled to push the door open with her hip and stepped inside the room to set the tray down on the table. In soft leather boots, she turned hastily to retreat.

"Wait!" Mandy held the girl by her upper arm. "Don't go. Stay and talk to me while I eat. If I don't talk to someone soon, I'll go crazy."

The girl hesitated. "Cook will miss me."

"Just for a little bit?" Mandy asked.

The girl glanced nervously at the two men in slick black armor who stood just outside the door. "Well, maybe for a minute."

"Guard the door, my armored friends!" Mandy said. Neither guard moved. How could she get away with guards at the door? She had to get away. Had to! Mandy's anger at her father flared, and she slammed the door. For the moment, she felt as if she had beaten her father at his own game. She turned to the girl and saw a look of fear on the girl's face. Mandy laughed trying to set the girl at ease. "Don't those guards make great statues?"

When the girl did not answer, Mandy ran around the table, pushing the chairs close. She gestured toward a chair and said, "Now, sit down."

The girl sat down, and Mandy handed a spoon to her and took the cover from a serving bowl of thick beef stew. She dipped a small portion of the stew onto a bread plate, then placed it in front of the girl and served herself on a saucer. Then she poured milk from a pitcher into a mug, placed it on the table next to the bread plate, and sat down.

"What's your name?" Mandy asked the girl.

"Gwenydd," she replied. She sat rigid in her seat, looking down at her plate.

"Well, Gwenydd," Mandy said, "how very nice to meet you. Now, you say that to me."

The girl looked at Mandy and back down at her plate. "Why?"

"Because," Mandy answered, "my grandmother said it's the proper thing to say at tea parties."

"Oh," Gwenydd said. She nervously slid her fingers toward the spoon but stopped short.

"Well," said Mandy growing impatient, "Are you going to say it?"

Gwenydd looked up again, and Mandy encouraged her with a nod of the head.

"How nice to meet you," Gwenydd said softly.

Mandy laughed and immediately wished she hadn't. Gwenydd looked as if she were on the verge of tears.

"Oh, I'm sorry, Lady Amanda. I did not mean to do it wrong."

"But you did it right, Gwenydd! I only laughed because I'm happy that we're playing together. I didn't mean to upset you." Mandy picked up her spoon and began to eat as Gwenydd grabbed a spoon and shoveled food into her mouth as fast as she could. Astonished that Gwenydd was so hungry, Mandy was annoyed with herself for wanting to play when Gwenydd needed to eat. Mandy leaned back in her chair and watched Gwenydd gulp the last of the milk from the mug. "Full?" Mandy asked.

"Not yet," Gwenydd said. "But there is no more."

"Yes, there is. Take mine," Mandy said and pushed her half-eaten stew over to Gwenydd.

Gwenydd's eyes widened. "I can't eat your food, Lady Amanda!"

"I'm not hungry, Gwenydd. If you don't eat it, then it will get thrown out."

Gwenydd grabbed the dish, and when she finished eating, she looked up at Mandy and laughed. "Oh, I have never tasted such good food!" she said.

Mandy dabbed the corner of her mouth with the napkin's edge and watched Gwenydd copy her. Then an idea came to Mandy. If Gwenydd lived at the Keep, then surely she would know how to get away. But would she help?

"I should get back to the kitchen now. Cook will be angry."

Mandy stood up. "Wait, Gwenydd. Please?"

In case the guards could hear them, Mandy took Gwenydd's hand and pulled her toward the balcony where she whispered, "I have to get out of here! I need to call my mother, and tell her I'm all right. But, my father won't let me leave. Help me, Gwenydd. Please?"

Gwenydd looked away. "Your father would beat me."

"No he wouldn't," Mandy said. "My father may be strict, and he's never beaten me." But Mandy wondered if he would beat someone else. She had never thought about that before and did not know the answer. "Help me, please?" Gwenydd kept her face turned away from Mandy.

"Oh, I could not!" She opened her mouth to say more, and then shut it as if she were afraid to speak.

Mandy touched Gwenydd's hands and turned her to look into her eyes. "Don't you see? I'd just tell him that I forced you to help me."

"You are his daughter. If I disobeyed him, he would beat me," Gwenydd said softly, and for some reason Mandy sensed truth in Gwenydd's statement. Her father had been acting more strange since he had been at the Keep.

"But what if he doesn't know who helped me?" Mandy asked. "I'll never tell him. And if I can get away and call my mother, she'll keep him away so he can't force me to tell!"

Mandy loosened her grip on Gwenydd's hands, but Gwenydd held tight. "You are sure she can do that?"

"I'm sure."

"Then how can I help?" Gwenydd asked.

"Do the guards stay outside my door all night?" Mandy asked.

"No, they go back to the barracks."

"Could you sneak back later and open the lock?"

"If I waited till the Midblack Bells. The bells ring so loud, you know ..."

"Say you can get back up here and unlock the door. Could you show me where I can find a phone?"

"A phone? I don't know what that is. But they have everything in the market at Keepsburg!"

"Is Keepsburg that village just outside the Keep?"

Gwenydd nodded.

Mandy had to go to the village to find a phone. But, people might notice that she was Kylasar's daughter wearing her own clothes. She looked out of place. Maybe she should dress like everybody else. Their clothes were *funny,* but she would look just as funny and no one would pay her any attention. "Could you find me clothes like you wear, Gwenydd?" Mandy pulled the leg of her jeans. "If I don't wear my blue jeans," she said then pointed to her shoes, "and sneakers, then I won't be noticed as Kylasar's daughter."

Gwenydd giggled, "Sneakers? To sneak around in?"

Mandy giggled, too. She gave Gwenydd a hug. "Can you find me clothes like yours to wear?"

"If I can sneak into the sewing room, I can get your own clothes. The seamstress and tanner have been working for days to make you some. Did you not know?"

Mandy had thought she would have to wear her jeans and T-shirt until they wore out. "No!" she replied. "Things are looking up. Now all you have to do is get my clothes and sneak back up here later. Then tell me how to get to Keepsburg, and I'll see if I can find a phone. Agreed?"

Gwenydd looked down. "I hate for you to go alone, Lady Amanda," she whispered.

"I'll be all right, Gwenydd. Don't worry," But, Mandy felt her stomach flip flop and did not feel as brave as she sounded. *Just don't get caught,* she thought glumly. If her father found out she deliberately disobeyed him, she would be in major trouble, big time.

CHAPTER TEN

WHILE TRACKING 'HORNES NEAR WHISPER-WOOD, THE GODS MAY COME TO CALL.

In the kitchen far below Mandy's tower room, Jorn hurried past the smell of fresh bread. He had no time to pluck a hot roll the cook offered from the paddle board pulled from the deep oven. Now that the Imperator was back (some people said he had traveled to other worlds) and bent on finding the One-Horne, Jorn would have to deal with the sorcerer's anger.

The Imperator had brought Jorn to the Keep to train him in the art of tracking. And he was good at tracking. Some said the best, but Jorn was not so sure. He had found hoof prints, yet had never seen the One-Horne, a horse with a golden horn that disappeared magically. And as far as Jorn was concerned, the One-Horne was like water on parched land.

Jorn worried about having to tell the Imperator that he had failed to find the animal, for he had heard rumors about the screams of those who had failed the Imperator. If Jorn were told to do something and balked, the rumor was that Imperator would not hesitate to kill him, and he preferred to keep his head, arms, and legs attached to his body. One rumor told about a scullery maid who refused to retire to Kylasar's room with him. The Imperator had pulled her long hair and had shaken her so hard that her neck had snapped. Jorn had not known anyone who had witnessed the act, but he had talked to those who had seen the guards removing her body.

Now, hesitating at the open doorway to the study, Jorn nervously watched the Imperator pace angrily back and forth in front of his cluttered work table, his heavy black robe sweeping behind him like a dark wave. The Imperator was a tall man who seemed to fill the room with weight and power. Kylasar turned and his shoulder-length dark-red hair framed dark brows over black eyes. His mouth wore a scowl. Jorn twisted his leather hat in hand and looked down to avoid the Imperator's glare. He dared not look into the oddly shaped glass jars of unimaginable moving things cluttering the work table. *Evil things*, Jorn remembered, and shuddered. Belanos, how much he had learned in the past years!

"You cannot find the One-Horne?" The Imperator growled. "Are you a tracker or an imbecile?"

Jorn winced. A large, reddish-brown spider scurried across the toe of his boot, and Jorn shivered and raised his eyes. "I am a tracker, sir, but tracking the One-Horne is like chasing one's shadow."

Kylasar's scowl was replaced by a smile that did not reach his eyes. His raised his shoulders and sighed. "Jorn, Jorn, I know it is hard, but you must find the One-Horne. It is imperative!"

Jorn grew confused. *The Imperator's demeanor had changed so suddenly. Could it be that the rumors about Kylasar's evil were untrue?*

Jorn shivered again. "I will."

From the mess on the cluttered, dust-ridden work table, the Imperator yanked open a parchment scroll and read. "The One-Horne was last seen around the Gargoyles of Gneiss." He carefully placed the scroll down on the table and picked up an arrow, the black shaft shimmering like quicksilver, the quill feathers glowing blood red, the tip flashing gold.

"Once you spot the One-Horne, shoot this arrow into the air. It will return, showing me where to find you. I will then come help you catch it."

Jorn wondered what magic spell the Imperator had placed on the arrow. If he touched it, would something happen to him? He looked into Kylasar's eyes.

"Go!" Kylasar whispered, and Jorn cautiously took the arrow and fled the room.

Later that evening, Jorn galloped on horseback east through Keepsburg on the Painted Path, a road of colored bricks forming pictures of beasts and men that legends said the gods made thousands of years before man had walked on Wry. The Painted Path ran straight through the bottom of a black rock canyon, which was cut between Shadowspawn Mountains edging the Midterranean Ocean on the western side of Wry. At the top of a hill, Jorn reined in his horse, Fluke. With a snort, the mare shook her golden mane and flicked her tail. Jorn patted her chestnut withers to calm her. If she became skittish, she could trip and break a leg. Below him, the Painted Path crumbled into a dirt road continuing east through Whisperwood Forest spreading out before him in the darkening twilight like a thick verdant tapestry.

Jorn knew that the Gargoyles were only a week's travel south across the foothills between Whisperwood Forest and Shadowspawn Mountains. But to Jorn, a week seemed too long. From the moment the arrow was in the quiver at his back, Jorn had felt something evil riding behind him looking over his shoulder. The sooner he found the One-Horne, the sooner he could get rid of the arrow.

So, he urged the horse, hooves clicking against the colored bricks, to the right. Heading south toward the Gargoyles, Jorn kneed Fluke around small boulders that dotted the lush green landscape and kept her gait steady. On his left and farther down the hill, Whisperwood Forest was a sinister shadow across the terrain. Its trees grew trunks too broad for Jorn to encircle with his arms, and leaves were so thick that no one could see what animals hid behind them. *I will not venture closer to the Forest than I have to*, he thought, eying the trees suspiciously. When the sun dipped behind the mountains and the shadows under the trees darkened to pitch, Fluke stumbled, and Jorn was forced to seek a place to stop for the night.

Finding shelter on the edge of Whisperwood Forest would be better than venturing into its menacing depths so close after sun-fall, he told himself. So when he came upon a small dip in the land where a fallen tree formed a good frame for a shelter, Jorn dismounted. The springy ground covered with pine straw would provide a soft place to sleep.

Jorn slid the saddle bags and blanket roll from the mare's back and then tossed them under the dead tree branches. He unstrapped the saddle and felt the horse blanket underneath soaked in sweat.

"Sorry, girl, " he crooned as he stroked Fluke's soft sides. "But we are going to have to travel hard to try again to find this One-Horne." He felt the near hopelessness of his task and shivered.

The horse snorted and leaned into Jorn's strokes. He looped her tether over the end of the dead tree, making sure that she had enough rope to graze.

Jorn gathered a few dried branches and hunted in his saddlebag for his sparking stones. Jorn could not afford to buy a faerlyte, but he did not think Belanos would mind him using fire. *It was only the priests who said using fire was blasphemy,* Jorn thought. They made up rules for reasons only they knew, and Jorn smiled when he thought that maybe their reasons amounted to greed. Only the church could sell craerlytes and faerlytes—making money to pay Kylasar for the use of his Rathriders and Black Guards. With them as enforcers, the priests had kept the ordinary people of Keepsburg in ignorance and poverty.

Once the fire blazed, he put a pan of water filled with tea spices over the fire and improvised a tent over the tree branches and a makeshift pallet of pine straw and a blanket. Jorn dug bread and cheese and a metal cup from the saddle bag. Later, he climbed under the tent and listened to the night filled with sounds of crickets, frogs, and night birds.

Later, he was startled from a deep, dreamless sleep by a nicker from Fluke. Hefting an axe, Jorn rolled quietly off the pallet and squatted on his heels. A soft rumble told him another horse was galloping in his direction. When Fluke neighed loudly, Jorn could have throttled her. Now whoever was coming would know that another rider was in the area. From a distance, Jorn heard a shill, ear-piercing whinny. Exhausted, he did not relish the thought of fighting an enemy. He wanted to flee, but he would look awfully stupid if the rider were someone he knew. Then again, what if the rider wasn't?

Fear spurred him across the moss-covered ground to Fluke's side. He pulled her head down to his. "Easy, girl," he whispered, but the horse tried to shake the halter from his hand. Frustrated by Fluke's fidgeting, Jorn jerked the halter harder than he intended. The leather halter strap slashed across his fingers, Fluke reared and bolted into the night.

"Fluke! Come back!" His shout echoed against the doubled thunder of hoof beats so close that he felt the ground vibrating under him. Surely the galloping horse would run over him in the dark. He blinked. The darkness brightened and a quiet settled over him, and light swept the ground in front of him. Jorn looked for the source of light and saw, some ten feet away, a flaring golden horn on the forehead of a huge, white horse wearing around its neck a medal held by a golden chain. With a long, white mane flowing around its body, the horse snuffed and pawed the ground. The One-Horne! Not believing his luck, he tried to remember where he had put Kylasar's arrow. But his mind seemed dull, full of fog, and all he could do was stare. The wondrous horse, at least two hands taller than Fluke, stared directly at Jorn with its blue eyes. He had never seen a horse with blue eyes. He felt his stomach lurch, then an empty feeling as if he were suddenly hungry for something that he had never tasted. The golden light brightened, and Jorn suddenly felt like crying. He had never seen an animal so beautiful, so graceful, so seemingly intelligent, and *good*. He wanted to touch it, to feel its velvety coat, to ride it into the night. Jorn decided he had to touch the horse. *Just once,* he thought, he had to touch it, and slowly, as if in a dream, he moved forward. The horse whinnied and danced backward. Jorn stopped and held his hand out. "Easy, boy." The white stallion pawed the ground, and Jorn concentrated on slowing his breathing, trying to project a calmness that he did not feel. "Easy," he said again and stepped closer.

With a whinny, the stallion pranced to a stand in front of Jorn. The light from the golden horn spread across Jorn's body, and he grew lightheaded. The horse lowered its head until Jorn could feel a warm breath move across his face, and the tip of the golden horn touch the top of his head. Golden light burst behind Jorn's eyes and sparked every nerve-ending in his body. He felt as if he had been struck by a bolt of golden lightning, as if he were bathed with warmth and goodness, as if he were in the presence of the gods, and he sank to his knees. The One-Horne was sacred, a horse worthy of the gods. Now he knew why the Imperator wanted it. He knew, too, that the Imperator would use the One-Horne in his foul magic. Jorn knew that now he would never shoot the arrow into the air.

The stallion pointed his horn at the ground where a faint, golden outline appeared in the air above the ground and formed the likeness of a young girl with dark eyes and hair. The stallion seemed to speak to him, *"Jorn, west of Shadowspawn Mountains far south of Keepsburg, this girl walks toward danger. Do not rest until she is safe, Jorn, safe from Imperator Kylasar."* The light that formed the girl twinkled into golden dust, and with a piercing whinny, the One-Horne raced into the night.

Stunned, Jorn wondered what he should do. There was no doubt that the One-Horne had been sent from Lord Dagda and Lady Brighid, and he would never be able to return to the Imperator's Keep. The Imperator would never let him live after finding out that Jorn had betrayed him and let the One-Horne go free. And who was the little girl that she needed protection from Kylasar? Could Jorn keep her safe from the Imperator? Could he even keep himself safe? After finding Fluke, he would get rid of the black arrow, for he dare not ride anywhere with it on his back. If Kylasar could home in on it, then he must stick the arrow in the ground. Jorn hefted the forgotten axe in his hand and, turning to go, was surprised to find his horse just behind him.

CHAPTER ELEVEN

THE BAND WITH POWERS OF WATER HELPS THE SEEKER TO SEE—

Katherine stood with Wren and Serhonydd, packs in hand, at the top of the hillfort looking out into the dark night. A cool breeze whipped around her, and she pulled her cloak tighter. In a leather pouch beneath her shirt, her father's lighter and the strange golden key lay tucked away. Although the euphoria she felt when she had first put on the Band of Brocoudahl had long since dissipated, she found that when she left it off for more than a few seconds, an excruciating headache throbbed against her temples and disappeared as soon as she put the band back on. Now, with feet comfortable in a pair of soft thigh-high boots, Katherine felt ready to tackle anything Wren, Serhonydd, and Shaeff wanted to throw her way. But, she thought, they had better not get in the way of her finding Mandy. That and only that was her first priority.

A blue-white light flared; Serhonydd held a craerlyte in his hand like a torch. He turned toward her.

"Are you ready, Katherine?" he asked. She nodded and Serhonydd spoke again. "Wren, is Shaeff coming?"

Wren nodded, put his fingers into his mouth, and whistled. Shaeff trotted up the dark hillside. "*Ready?*" he asked.

Serhonydd nodded. "All right, let's go."

Shaeff, tail wagging, bounced past Serhonydd to lead them down the hill. Silver moonlight mixed with the light from the craerlyte and rippled across an almost straight path along the eastern bank of the Ridge River. Katherine, a step behind Serhonydd, heard running water and smelled dampness in the air. Wren had said that they were headed north toward a waterfall that emptied down a thousand-foot rock cliff into the river from the Sea of Silk.

"How far to Wry's Ken?" Katherine asked.

"Wry's Ken sits four to five days northwest of us," Serhonydd replied, "between the banks of the Sea of Silk and the western range of the Black Ridge Mountains."

If the Ridge River ran north and Wry's Ken was also to the north, then Katherine wondered aloud, "Why not go by boat?"

Serhonydd answered, "The current flows from north to the south too fast to row against. We will probably return by river. That is, if we are able to return."

If we return? Katherine's heart quickened. Perhaps he only meant that the Blue Sorcerers would know where to find Mandy, and if not, they would send her to someone who did. Afraid that she would start worrying again, Katherine forced her attention to the path.

The dark shapes of the Fogfiend Mountains loomed above her on the right. She looked for the river on her left but saw only shoulder-high grass. *Four or five days of walking through this?* Modern civilization, with its cars, trains, and buses, was a distinct disadvantage to keeping one fit, Katherine realized, as she watched Serhonydd moving gracefully down the slight incline. He seemed so brusque with her that she wondered why he was helping her. Why was he taking her to the Blue Sorcerers? Katherine wished that Wren had not taken her to meet Serhonydd. She did not trust him.

Serhonydd gestured with the craerlyte toward a small circular sandy clearing off the path on their left. "We will rest and eat."

Katherine dropped her pack and sat.

"Do not get too comfortable," Serhonydd said, "we're only stopping to eat."

Katherine grimaced. "I thought it was too good to last."

Serhonydd smiled and placed the craerlyte into the soft dirt. Through the shimmering blue, Serhonydd's eyes met hers. Knowing that she had probably looked stupid, and to keep from embarrassing herself more, Katherine turned to look for Shaeff.

After eating, Katherine thought she heard a strange sound like a sheet on a clothesline flapping in the wind. Shaeff raced into the clearing and Serhonydd was on his feet. "Get the packs, Wren. *NOW.*" He grabbed the craerlyte and pushed everything back into his pack.

Katherine rose to her feet. "What's wrong?" Shaeff prodded Katherine with his nose.

"*DANGER COMES!*" Shaeff's thought screamed in her head, and he disappeared into the tall thick grass toward the riverbank. Serhonydd grabbed Katherine's arm and pulled her behind him, stumbling toward the water. She slid on the dew-covered grass and Serhonydd tightened his grip on her arm. Katherine did not understand what was wrong, but the flapping sounds grew louder, and in the darkness, the air pulsated like a storm brewing. Whatever made the noise had to be huge, she thought, then Serhonydd pulled her down, forcing her flat in the tall grass.

"Make no sound," he hissed.

Katherine tried hard to ease her ragged breathing. She shivered, teeth chattering, and clamped her mouth shut. She closed her eyes and on the back of her eyelids, a dark shape soared closer, spinning, dissolving into a monstrous, bat-like creature with leathery wings. She did not know if the Band of Brocoudahl or Shaeff projected the image. All she knew was that she seemed to be able mentally to see what flew over her in the ink-black sky. That image was like no nightmare she had ever had. Its eyes were empty sockets and razor-sharp teeth filled a cavernous mouth. Upon the monster's back another being rode like an evil shadow, exuding putrefaction like a black aura. She dared not breathe and tried to shrink inside herself. But now the terrible beasts were directly above, and a banshee scream shattered the night. Katherine prayed that she would wake up, safe at home.

Suddenly, the beasts seemed to vanish from her internal sight. She opened her eyes and Serhonydd peered closely into her face. "You all right?" he asked.

"I ... think so," she shuddered. "What was it?"

"You could see it?" Serhonydd sounded incredulous.

"Not with my eyes." She shook her head trying to erase the image from her mind. "It was what I thought it looked like, but maybe I just imagined it."

"No," Serhonydd whispered harshly, "not your imagination. The Band of Brocoudahl gave you the power to see the shape of evil." He gently touched her cheek and smiled absently.

"It was a Rathrider. A sentinel belonging to Kylasar," he said. Behind him, Wren appeared, his eyes white with fright.

"Was it looking for me?" Katherine asked softly.

"Perhaps, for it is only a matter of time before Kylasar discovers you are on Wry, Katherine. The Rathriders will come looking for you."

CHAPTER TWELVE

O CHILDE, BEWARE IN DARKEST NIGHT, THE TOWERS DRESS IN BLACK.

A bolt clanging turned Mandy's thoughts toward the massive prison door. "Gwenydd," she whispered, "Is that you?"

The door opened, and Gwenydd slipped inside. "Yes, Lady Amanda. It's me." She handed a cloth bundle to Mandy. "Here are your clothes."

"Great!" Gwenydd had brought her a white dress-like a petticoat with a gathered neck and puffed sleeves and what looked like a long leather rectangle with a hole in the middle. The leather felt as soft as her mother's kidskin gloves and fell to her knees over the petticoat.

Gwenydd handed her a strip of leather, "Tie this around your waist to hold the jerkin in place." Gwenydd pulled out a pair of leather boots. Mandy tugged them on. Then Gwenydd handed Mandy a coarse, woolen cape with a hood.

Mandy grabbed up her Nikes, jeans, and T-shirt and shoved them under the covers. She turned to Gwenydd. "Now I'm ready to go!"

Gwenydd opened the door slowly and peeked out. "All is quiet, Lady Amanda."

Outside the tower room, Mandy relocked the door behind them, glad to be free.

By the light of a metal-bracketed craerlyte set into the wall behind them, Mandy followed Gwenydd down stone steps leading into darkness. Her father would be upset, but she thought, he could not be too angry with her for wanting to call her mother. And besides, it would serve him right for locking her in.

Mandy remembered the trek up the steps to the tower prison as much shorter, but now the spiraling descent seemed to go on forever into darkness, broken occasionally by moonlight trickling through narrow slits in the stone walls. She could hear her boots against the steps and the soft sound of her own breathing. The steps ended at a door with an iron ring anchored in its middle. "On the other side of this door," Gwenydd whispered, "we must cross the courtyard to the left of the servants' quarters, where steps will take us up on the wall. There we'll hide until the guards lower the drawbridge in the morning."

"What do you mean, we'll hide?" Mandy hissed. "You've got to get back to your room so my father won't know you've helped me. Remember? We made a deal."

Gwenydd laughed softly.

"What are you laughing at, Gwenydd?"

"Shh! I'm going with you. I'd rather go with you than stay here by myself."

Mandy didn't know whether or not to be glad that Gwenydd was going with her. Sure, she could use the company but, Mandy wondered, would it get Gwenydd in trouble with her father? Gwenydd carefully twisted the iron ring, pushed the door open, and squirmed through the open doorway. She motioned Mandy to follow.

Over the courtyard and far above the wall, stars twinkled in the dark. It felt good to be free. A cobblestone walk led from the wooden door through a short grassy courtyard directly in front of Mandy to a single-story servants' quarters against a dark wall of the Keep. Light glowed through a window in the building, and Mandy could hear faint laughter and talk.

Then a door banged open and Mandy and Gwenydd froze like startled rabbits. Light spilled from the servant's quarters across the cobblestone walk only inches from Gwenydd's feet. A guard stood in the building's doorway.

"Ah-ha! I've got you now!"

Mandy held her breath.

Then a feminine voice teased, "If you think you've got me, then come get me!"

The guard stepped into the building and slammed the door. The light vanished from the grass and, seconds later, disappeared from the window.

"That was close!" Mandy whispered.

Gwenydd turned, clasped Mandy's hand, and dashed to the left side of the building and up stone steps to the top of the Keep wall.

Keeping to the inside edge against a three-foot-high parapet, where the starlight failed to lighten the shadows, they pattered across the rampart, their feet like secret whispers slapping the flagstones.

In front of them, the first tower rose, a huge blackness that blotted out the star-studded sky. When Gwenydd paused, Mandy thought that they'd been found out. "What's wrong?" she asked.

Gwenydd shivered. "Without light, we can't enter the tower. We could pitch head first down the stairs."

"Are the stairs next to the wall?"

"I don't remember." Mandy felt Gwenydd's frustration.

"Well, we're not going back now, so come on." Mandy eased around Gwenydd, put out her hand and felt past the opening to the wall on the right of the tower. The wall felt cold and damp. Carefully hugging the wall, she slid one foot forward into the tower. She patted the floor with her foot, found the floor to be solid and then moved, one foot-sliding step at a time, deeper into the darkness with her right hand trailing the wall. Mandy reached her left hand back to feel for Gwenydd's hand. "Come on, Gwenydd. Take my hand. It's all right." The two girls, hand in hand, moved across the tower floor.

Through the tower and back on the rampart, they moved with more confidence to the second tower, smaller than the first, Mandy still in front. Halfway around the tower's wall, Mandy peeked out a window open to the night sky stitching starlight to a tall mountain range and discovered that the tower looked down over an endless pool of black. "Where's the drawbridge?" she asked.

Gwenydd looked down. "It's up. Otherwise you'd see lights across the chasm. We can hide until morning, when the guards let the drawbridge down. Then with the people heading to Keepsburg, we can walk out unnoticed."

"But where do we hide?"

"Follow me." Gwenydd led them down the steps to the bottom of the tower. She moved behind the spiral steps. "It's empty!" she whispered. "Come on!"

Mandy hunched down and entered a dark crawl space. She could not see a thing in the pitch-blackness and jumped when Gwenydd's hand touched her shoulder.

"Sit down," Gwenydd said, and Mandy edged close to the back wall. It was cold, and she shivered. She could barely discern a grayer space where they had entered the crawl space, but she sat down and felt Gwenydd sitting next to her.

"It's so dark," Mandy said. "Now what do we do?"

"Get some sleep."

"Shouldn't one of us stay awake, like a lookout or something?"

"I suppose I could stay awake for a bit," Gwenydd answered. "Then I'll wake you up when I get sleepy so you can keep a lookout."

"Okay, Gwenydd. Good night." Mandy wrapped her cape close. Lying on her side, she thought, *I probably won't be able to sleep.*

The next thing Mandy knew, someone was shaking her.

"I can't keep my eyes open anymore," Gwenydd whispered.

Slowly, Mandy remembered where she was. "All right," she said. "Go to sleep." Gwenydd lied down next to her and Mandy sat up. She wanted to stand up to stretch her cramped legs but was afraid she would make too much noise. She sat back against the wall and listened to the night. Every now and then, she could hear somebody calling out that all was well, but the voice was always distant. At one point, she dozed and dreamed that her father was two men, one shining like an angel all in white and the other, all green and glowing like a Martian. She tried to grab their hands to pull them back together, but the man in white shattered like an image in a mirror. She tried to scoop up the broken shards, and the green man laughed and spun away from her outstretched hand.

Her head jerked against the cave wall and she woke up, crying. It was a strange dream, she thought, and one she didn't want to dream again. After wiping the tears from her eyes, she could see Gwenydd curled beside her. A pre-dawn light appeared outside with the smell of bacon blossoming through the air, reminding her that she had not thought to bring along any provisions. *We don't even have water to drink,* she thought. *How stupid!*

"Gwenydd!" Mandy whispered and shook the girl gently.

"What?" Gwenydd sat up quickly, wide awake in an instant.

"We didn't bring any food or water along. We're going to starve!"

From under her cape, Gwenydd brought a black coin.

"I did not dare steal anything from the kitchen, but I have this coin that I found last year." Gwenydd put the coin into Mandy's hand. "You can buy food and water for us in the marketplace."

"Why can't you keep it?"

"Because they would think that I had stolen it. No one will question you with coin, for you do not look like a servant with your new clothes."

"If we come back to the Keep, I'll get the money from my father to repay you."

Gwenydd's eyes opened wide.

"No, Lady Amanda! I don't need the coin back. It was mere chance that I came by it!"

There it was again, Mandy thought. Why was Gwenydd so frightened whenever Mandy mentioned her father? Gwenydd knew something that she was not telling. Maybe she would tell her later, when they were better friends.

There was a horrendous sound of gears cranking, chains clanking.

"They're lowering the drawbridge," Gwenydd whispered.

They had to move.

"Come on, Gwenydd; we'd better get going." She clutched the coin tightly in her hand and scooted from the crawl space. Gwenydd edged up beside her, and together, they left the tower.

The sun was not quite up, but pink clouds were smeared against a purple-gray background in the little bit of sky they could see above the Keep walls. Trailing down the walls, ivy glistening with dew, they came to an inner courtyard of flagstones rubbed smooth from years of scuffling human feet and prancing horse hooves. Across the courtyard and twenty feet away from where Mandy stood, two iron doors, each as big as a double garage door, were set into a wall with a large tower at either end. When the doors opened, four guards in black marched across the flagstones to a portcullis on Mandy's right. The guards disappeared under the portcullis, and the sounds of metal rubbing against metal stopped with a thud. More guards marched from the iron doors and people bustled out of the Keep toward the drawbridge. Carts filled with straw and barrels of fruit and vegetables rumbled across the oak planks of the lowered drawbridge, bounced through the open gates, and creaked over the flagstone.

"All right," Gwenydd said. "Walk slowly and keep your head down. Nobody will notice us."

"I hope not," Mandy whispered. She prayed that if the guards captured them, Gwenydd would be all right. Mandy imagined her father, angry at their escape, slapping Gwenydd and tossing Mandy back in the tower prison. Would she be able to pacify her father or would he react like a stranger? Mandy worried that Gwenydd might be right in thinking that she would be in bad trouble.

The two girls slipped from the beneath the tower steps into the confusion of the crowd. Mandy covered her head with the cape's hood and followed Gwenydd under the huge portcullis. She wanted to look up, but she was afraid that one of the guards standing watch across the portcullis would spot her. Once outside the gate and upon the wooden drawbridge, she noticed that on either side of the wide walkway was a long drop off into empty space. She had no idea how high up she was, but the side rails did not look very strong, and the other end of the drawbridge seemed far away. She had not been afraid crossing the drawbridge when riding the horse with her father, but that had been different. Now she could see the sea swirling far below through the chinks between the boards, and she drew in a breath of terror and moved closer to Gwenydd.

CHAPTER THIRTEEN

O CHILDE BE LEERY, DANGER LURKS, AND FINDS YOU UNAWARE.

Once across the drawbridge, Mandy breathed easier. The early morning sky had turned from pink to a clear French blue with small tendrils of white clouds. Birds sang from the bushes inset along the walls on both sides of what her father had called the Painted Path. Above the walls, bare black rock cliffs jutted straight up into huge mountains.

Men, women, and children walked with baskets loaded with fruit and vegetables. Some headed toward the Keep, while others ambled toward town. Many had on dull brown shifts, others wore pants with vests and no shirts, and all appeared dirty and hungry, their eyes surrounded by dark circles. The children were silent, and even the adults talked very little.

"Gwenydd," she whispered, "why is everyone so quiet?" Gwenydd shrugged.

"There's Keepsburg," she said, and pointed down the road to the village Mandy had ridden through with her father, but then Mandy's eyes had been on the Keep. Now she saw dirty, clay-colored houses too poor and dilapidated to have telephones. Mandy could not see any telephone poles. Maybe the lines were buried. The dull houses had open doorways and few windows. Mandy caught a whiff of something rotten and noticed children running through a pile of decaying fruit and vegetables heaped between two houses at the edge of the roadway. One little boy, about four years old, sat in the middle throwing rocks at a large, brown rat. Mandy shivered. Beggars sat inside doorways and stared at her as she passed.

"Where are we going, Gwenydd?" she asked.

"To the market," Gwenydd replied.

"I hope the market is cleaner than this," Mandy mumbled.

"Oh, it is."

Mandy tried to smile, but she knew that her mouth was set in disgust. She could not wait to find a phone and call her mother. She did not have much time before the guards would find her room empty. They could already be out looking for her.

They came to a large square filled with people haggling over prices, hurrying from one side of the street to the other, calling out to each other under doorways with wooden signs painted with pictures of sheep, cows, books, bottles in odd shapes, and a spoon and fork. Wooden stalls with racks of apples and oranges, kegs of fish, hangers with bright scarves, trays of silver and gold trinkets, stacked swords and tables with feathers, arrows, and knives, filled the square in front of the shops. But there were no cars, no television antennas, no metal buildings, nothing that resembled Akron. Keepsburg was the strangest place Mandy had ever seen.

A fat woman smoothed her stubby fingers across a bolt of sky blue silk, told the man behind the counter that its quality was poor, and that she would only give him two dinas for it. He spit on the ground and laughed and said it was worth ten. The woman puffed up her enormous bulk and stalked away, muttering. Mandy heard a loud shout and then spun to see a thin man fling a large knife at a dark fellow standing against a wooden wall. The knife thudded deep into the wood next to his neck and the dark man grinned, showing a row of crooked, dark teeth, and turned and pulled the knife out of the soft wood.

"Throwing knives fer sale!" he growled, and as he tossed the knife back to its owner, people clapped. By now, an audience had gathered to follow him toward the stall where his partner waited.

"Boy," said Mandy. "I thought he was trying to kill the other guy!"

Gwenydd laughed.

"They do it all the time! Come, Mandy. Let's get something to eat!" and she walked quickly into the market. Mandy, following close behind, was thinking that they should try to find a telephone, but at a stall radiating the aroma of bacon, Gwenydd stopped. A lady behind the counter poked bacon frying on a red-orange craerlyte, then turned to a stack of thin, flat looking hot cakes and placed two next to the bacon on the hot crystal.

"Tell her we want two bacon cakes, Mandy."

Mandy put up two fingers and the lady wrapped two cakes in a coarse brown paper.

Mandy handed her the black coin and the woman looked closer at Mandy, placed some silver coins into Mandy's empty hand, and handed the bacon cake bundles to Mandy.

"Come on!" Gwenydd hissed.

Mandy handed Gwenydd a bacon cake and bit into her own. At another stall, they bought a watered-down fruit drink in a short bamboo tube.

"I cannot understand why I have not seen a telephone pole," Mandy mumbled.

"What?" asked Gwenydd.

"I can't find a telephone."

Gwenydd looked at her with her serious hazel eyes.

"I have never heard that word before."

Mandy sighed.

"A telephone is so big," she moved her hands together to indicate size, "and has buttons on it. You push the number of the person you want, and when that person picks up the telephone, you can talk to her."

Gwenydd smiled.

"You mean you can talk to your mother when she's not here?"

"Yes!"

Gwenydd clapped her hands together and laughed.

"Then I know what a telephone is!"

Mandy smiled. Things were going to work out all right after all.

Looking quite pleased with herself, Gwenydd announced, "It is a magic spell!"

Maybe Gwenydd had lived in the Keep for so long that she had never seen or used a phone.

"No, Gwenydd. A phone is not a spell. It's real."

Perhaps the village was too small to have phone service.

"Is Keepsburg the biggest village around?" Mandy asked.

"I've heard tell of a village run by the Dru'damen east of here, called Wry's Ken. It is said to be a very strange place."

"How so?" Mandy asked.

"People say the sun sparkles off tall towers made of blue stone, and there are strange-colored carts without wheels that move across water and carry people to strange places …"

"Move!" a voice intruded. Mandy turned to see a guard poke his sword at a small boy. The boy raced away, and Mandy pulled Gwenydd behind a jewelry stall, and poked her head past the stall's wooden back wall. More guards, their heavy-booted feet pounding across the street, followed close behind the first, scuffling around the area in front of the stall, and appearing angry. Had her guards discovered she was not in the tower prison?

One of the guards yelled to the people moving away.

"Gold dinas to anyone knowing the whereabouts of Lady Amanda Kylasar!" The woman who sold them bacon cakes turned back to the guard. Her eyes were dark, and she looked as if talking to the guard was something she loathed doing. *Oh no,* Mandy thought, *she is going to tell him that she's seen me!*

"What's she look like?" the woman asked.

The guard held his sword out flat at Mandy's height.

"She's about so high, and she has long dark hair braided down the middle of her back and brown eyes. She's ten sun-trips old."

"What's she done?" the woman asked.

The guard looked puzzled for a moment.

"Done? She's run off from her father, Imperator Kylasar, that's what she's done!" His voice rose in anger. "Have you seen her?"

The woman smoothed her apron with her hands. "Not me," she answered and turned and walked away.

Mandy could not believe her good fortune, but why would the woman want to protect her from the guards? They merely wanted to return her to her father. Wouldn't the woman want her safe at home with her father? Mandy wondered, and then a blow struck her on the back of the head and bright white stars erupted around her.

CHAPTER FOURTEEN

WHILE EVIL PLOTS A DARK REVENGE, THE CHILDE SLIPS FROM HIS GRASP.

A knock sounded on the study door. Kylasar, tired from being up most of the night and angry at being disturbed, rose from his chair in front of the fireplace with its ashes long cold. Captain Bevel stood nervously looking down at his feet. Kylasar glared. "What is it now?"

"Lady Amanda is gone, sir," Bevel said.

Kylasar grabbed the guard's forearm.

"I don't think I heard you," he hissed. Bevel kept his eyes averted.

"Your daughter has escaped her room, sir."

He could not believe that Amanda had the mettle to escape. *She was not capable of such a thing!* Kylasar thrust the man away and stomped back into the study to pace in front of the dead fire. He wanted to hit something, anything. *"Can you not even hold your daughter, human?"* Loche sneered.

"Shut up!" Kylasar said.

"Sir?" Bevel asked.

"Not you, you dolt." Kylasar stopped his pacing. Since Amanda did not know her way around the Keep, maybe she was just hiding from him and sulking. She wanted to go home. Maybe this was her way of making him send her home. *"Most unlikely,"* Loche said, and Kylasar agreed. She could be such a nuisance at times. Even when he found her, he certainly would not let her go home.

"Sir," Bevel said, "We found no trace of them. I think she went to Keepsburg."

"Why do you think that?"

"I found her strange clothes under her bedcovers. A serving girl has disappeared, and when I questioned the guards on the drawbridge, they said soon after they lowered the drawbridge, two youngsters headed toward Keepsburg. I and five of my men went to Keepsburg to bring them back."

Kylasar pressed his sharp fingernail against the skin below Bevel's ear. "If she is not found before sunset, you will forfeit your captaincy. And, maybe your head. Do you understand?"

"Yes, sir."

Kylasar lightly scratched Bevel's cheek with his fingernail and dismissed him, and then shut his eyes and rubbed his forehead with his fingers. *Couldn't anyone do anything right?*

CHAPTER FIFTEEN

HOLD TO THE POWERS OF SPIRIT—
OVER THE RAINBOW TRAIL.

On the fourth full day after leaving Crystal Caer, Katherine stopped on the wet, slippery trail. The sun was slowly descending on her left, and a cool evening breeze whipped over her. The Fogfiend mountains, which had hugged the horizon along the eastern side of the trail, now rose in front of her to join a western range Serhonydd had called the Black Ridge Mountains. Dark stitches across the orange sunset, the Black Ridge Mountains tumbled into knobby hills and grassy plains that ended at the western bank of the Ridge River, now some hundred feet below the spot where Katherine stood. North in the distance and above her line of vision, the river sliced a deep cleft between the Black Ridge and Fogfiend Mountains. Tons of water falling a thousand feet created a waterfall so powerful that she could hear its thunder and feel its moisture even here, at least a mile away. Where the wall of water cascaded down into the chasm, lush silver green ferns hung from crevices on either side of the falls. Rays from the setting sun bounced rainbows off boulders wet with spray and sparkled like silver glitter tossed into the air.

The waterfall was their destination, and she shivered thinking how dangerous and slick the steepening trail would become.

Serhonydd was in front of her, easing along a narrow ledge in a rock cliff face that plummeted to a cauldron of churning white water in the river far below. Shaeff, who had stayed close to Katherine since the night the Rathrider had passed overhead, now bumped against her leg. For comfort, she reached down to pat his silver fur and then moved forward.

After what seemed like hours, Serhonydd stopped on the ledge and pointed to where the trail ended in a circle of trees, with periwinkle blue and silver leaves sparkling like jewels atop brown velvet moss-covered trunks. Behind the trees, rock-cut ledges rose into mountains on the right. On the left, the falls, catching the last rays from the setting sun, rose above her. Katherine judged that they were about a third of the distance down from the top of the falls. *Much too high,* she thought.

Serhonydd said something. She could not hear over the tons of crashing water. "What?" she shouted. Serhonydd pointed to Shaeff.

"Serhonydd says we will rest here."

Katherine did not think she would like spending the night in the dampness.

"There is a Hide-hut," Shaeff interrupted. *"Serhonydd will show you."*

Serhonydd walked between two trees and with a quick movement ran his hand over the rough surface of the rock face. A rock door swung back and Shaeff ran past Serhonydd into the dark opening. When the dog padded back, Serhonydd beckoned to Katherine and Wren. Wren handed Serhonydd a craerlyte, which he turned into blue-white light. Serhonydd entered the cave-like opening with Katherine and Wren close behind.

The rock door swung swiftly shut behind them and left them in silence. Serhonydd stuck the craerlyte into soft dirt in the middle of the cave. In the blue-white glow, Katherine saw that the cave walls were made from the same black basalt of the hillfort entranceway. Wren pulled damp and musty mats down from a stack against the wall. Each of them settled onto a mat. Katherine shrugged the cape off her shoulders. The cave felt warm.

"Well," she said softly, "At least we can hear."

Serhonydd smiled.

After they had eaten, Serhonydd said, "Tomorrow we will cross the river."

"How?" Katherine interrupted.

Serhonydd glared. "If I may finish?"

She dropped her eyes, angry that he had made her feel stupid.

"Tomorrow," he continued, "will be soon enough to tell you how. We sleep now to be fully rested come sun-strike."

Serhonydd and Wren bedded down for the night. Katherine avoided looking at Serhonydd, but silently seethed inside. She curled up on her musty mat with her back to him, thinking that if his attitude didn't change for the better, she would end up telling him off. He had no right to talk to her the way he did. She had a right to know what he was planning to do. After all, it was Mandy that they were searching for. And she would not allow anybody to interfere with her finding her daughter. Least of all, an arrogant Dru'dammen. She felt Shaeff snuggle against her back. Too tired to stay awake, Katherine joined him in dreamless slumber.

She awoke to Serhonydd's nudge and ate the dried fruit that he handed her.

"The way across the Ridge River runs behind the waterfall and is treacherous, wet, and slick," Serhonydd said. "The noise is unbearable, so we will first pack our ears with clay, then rely on sight and touch for our safety." Serhonydd handed her two tar-black clay plugs. "We will keep to the same order as our trek on the path, except Shaeff will bring up the rear. If at any time, you feel that you are slipping, drop to your hands and knees. Do not panic." He looked steadily into Katherine's eyes. She thought the way must be extremely dangerous and, not sure that she could do it, fought down the urge to laugh hysterically.

She pushed the plugs into her ears to muffle the roar of the falls and followed Serhonydd back to the edge of a sheer vertical drop. The waterfall, an avalanche of blue water, spewed over the top some two hundred feet above her and crashed past to plunge a thousand feet to the bottom of the chasm. A narrow ledge carved into the side of the cliff that she was standing on disappeared behind the waterfall. Spray danced across the ledge and turned its jagged surfaces into wet mirrors that reflected rainbows and blue water. Katherine trembled from the sheer mass of water plunging before her. Maybe they should go back and find another way to cross Ridge River.

Wren and Serhonydd adjusted their earplugs and secured their leather bags over their shoulders, and then Serhonydd nimbly stepped onto the ledge and motioned for Katherine to follow. She felt lightheaded. There was no hand rail to hold onto, and the ledge was not wide enough to hold both her and Serhonydd. She would knock them off, and they would fall a thousand feet to be crushed under tons of pounding water on the rocks far below. Rooted at the edge, she shook her head. Her legs would not budge.

Shaeff rubbed up against her. *"The quicker you start, the sooner the journey ends."*

"I know," she thought, *"but I'm afraid."*

"Just go slowly. We are all here to help."

Shaeff's confidence surged into her mind, and Katherine felt the lightheadedness ease. On the ledge, Serhonydd looked at her and his eyes, as blue as the water pouring down behind him, seemed to send her courage. Serhonydd held his hands up, and she leaned forward, intertwining her fingers with his, and she carefully slid her feet onto the ledge. The ear plugs softened the roar of the falls, but Katherine could still feel a rumble through the soles of her feet, and the air vibrated with pressure. She turned back in time to see Wren and Shaeff follow her. Then Serhonydd released her hands. Turning back to Serhonydd, Katherine watched as he eased carefully along the ledge into a dark tunnel. A solid blue curtain of water was on his left and a jagged wall was on his right, curving into a ceiling above. The murky air was filled with a fine mist, and Katherine could not see far in the darkness. She wondered how they would see to cross the ledge, and then from his pack Serhonydd pulled and lit the craerlyte. Its blue glow reflected on water droplets and lit the darkness with an eerie sheen; Serhonydd nimbly stepped deeper into the tunnel and turned and beckoned to her. Katherine stepped hesitantly onto the slick surface.

She slid her hand along the wet rock wall on her right and carefully edged one foot forward and then slid her other foot up to meet it. The rock wall felt like a stone covered with moss on the bottom of a stream. She moved forward, following Serhonydd and the glow from the craerlyte. Her foot slipped, and she hugged the wall for a moment until her heartbeat returned to normal. If she had tripped near the edge, she thought, the force of the water would have snatched her from the ledge. She looked back and saw Wren and Shaeff moving toward her. With an odd taste of salt in her mouth mixed with the smell of sulfur, Katherine tried to swallow and turned back to proceed in Serhonydd's direction. He was far into the blue-black tunnel. Katherine glanced toward the wall of water that glowed from without. *The sun must be rising outside,* she thought, *but it is still dark and damp here, and the tunnel seems to go on forever.*

Katherine did not know how long she had been moving across the ledge when her foot slid out from under her and she fell heavily, a jagged edge of rock stabbing into her knee. Pain flashed through her leg, and she cried out. Blinking tears back, she watched Serhonydd continue slowly across the rock ledge to step onto a large, flat boulder surrounded in sunlight. Silver-green plants grew behind the boulder on the rock face. With the clay ear plugs in place, he had not heard her cry out. She did not know if she could stand up, the pain was so bad. Wren arrived behind her and gently pulled her up and draped her left arm around his shoulder. With Katherine hobbling and putting little pressure on her leg, they moved toward Serhonydd.

Just a little further, she told herself . . . *almost there* . . . and then they reached the boulder. Wren eased Katherine down under blue sky and when Shaeff trotted surefooted across the shelf with the skill natural to his species and jumped on the boulder, Katherine smiled. Serhonydd nodded to her as if he had had no doubts about them making it across, but Wren pointed to her leg, allowing her a chance to pull her pants leg up to inspect the wound. Her knee was not cut, only badly bruised, but it hurt. Wren startled her by applying a clear balm to the wound. Almost immediately, the pain diminished and as she watched, the balm absorbed the skin's purple discoloration, puffed up into a bead, then rolled from her leg on to Wren's fingers. He placed the bead into his bag, offered her a hand, and helped her up. The knee felt fine. After they removed their ear plugs, Katherine asked, "What was that, Wren?"

"Nothing special, just an ointment."

"Well, it worked wonders." Leaning gratefully on Wren, Katherine tested standing on her leg then carefully moved to follow Serhonydd up steps cut into the rocks above the boulder. By the time she reached the top, Katherine knew her leg was fine.

She stood on the west side of Ridge River with Wren and Shaeff beside her. To her right, a saffron-colored sea emptied its waters into the falls. Above and to her left, the Black Ridge Mountains rose in jagged, purple peaks awash with light from the morning sun. Serhonydd trudged down a northwesterly path that reminded her of a toboggan run edged with yellow, red, and blue wild flowers spread over silver-green grass.

Katherine called, "Serhonydd! Wait!"

Serhonydd stopped and turned. His eyes flashed irritation.

"I need a break," Katherine said. "Just for a minute, please?"

His now steel-blue eyes connected with hers: "The longer you rest, Katherine, the longer it will be before we find your daughter."

CHAPTER SIXTEEN

O' WAYWARD SON, THE TIME IS NIGH TO FACE YOUR DARKEST FEARS—

Serhonydd continued down the steep path toward Wry's Ken. Purple granite cliffs rose into the Black Ridge Mountains on his left. He watched the golden seagulls soar shrieking into the crisp blue sky and riding on warm air pockets above the Sea of Silk hundreds of feet below on his right. The air smelled of the sea, and Serhonydd could taste salt. A bird dove deep into the sea and brought up a fish in its beak.

In single file, Katherine, Wren, and Shaeff walked behind Serhonydd, who did not want to look at Katherine too much. His heart seemed to beat a little faster when he looked into her eyes, the same jade green of the elder plant. This strange new feeling disturbed him.

Now he paused in the path. Far below, Wry's Ken sat in a narrow valley between the Black Ridge Mountains and the Sea of Silk. *Home,* he thought, but he doubted that his parents, Lady A'legra and Lord A'leron, the two most revered among the Blue Circle, would welcome him after his years spent in the hermitage. Would they be ashamed of him, thinking he had been in hiding from Kylasar? Or thinking he had rebelled from their teachings? Would they turn him away? He did not know, but how they reacted to him would be of no importance. Now that

Imperator Kylasar was back in residence at the Keep, the Dru'dammen and Yttoshamen people were once again at risk. Serhonydd would not risk their deaths because of his own pride. If the Seeker did not find her loss on Wry, the world would end. Katherine was the Seeker that the chronicles foretold would come to Wry, and she needed help to find her daughter. He had to take her to his parents.

He turned back to Katherine standing beside him, looking down upon Wry. She was not as beautiful as some women he had known. But her oval face and almond-shaped eyes, lined by long auburn lashes, seemed to hold him in thrall. She turned to meet his gaze, and he read in her eyes that she had known grief and pain.

She smiled at him and suddenly turned to say something to Wren. He let his thoughts wander back to the upcoming confrontation with his parents. *Belanos,* he thought, *I dread this.*

CHAPTER SEVENTEEN

O'WARE THE STRANGERS' VILE INTENT TO SPIRIT ALL AWAY.

Mandy opened her eyes on two dusty reddish-brown legs that tapered into cracked, gray hooves clopping on rock-strewn dirt. Her head throbbed, her legs were numb, and her stomach felt queasy from the smell of the coarse-furred animal that jolted her stomach with every step it took. Turning her head, Mandy saw a long, furry ear twitch at buzzing purple horseflies. *A donkey,* she thought. I've *been flung over a donkey's back.* She tried to move her arms hanging below her head, and discovered that her arms and legs were strapped together under the animal's belly. Why was she tied up? Only kidnappers tied up children, she thought. Had they kidnapped her? To hold her for ransom? But Father wasn't rich and neither was Mother, she thought. She had to get away, but how?

Where is Gwenydd? she wondered. She could hear the hooves of more than one animal and now and then, grunts and hard breathing sounded with clinks and rattles close by. She wanted to open her eyes to look around again, but the back of her eyes hurt. *Probably from the knock on the head,* she thought. Then the donkey stumbled. She heard a sharp crack, an undecipherable oath, and a man's voice said, "Dumb beast, move on!"

The donkey brayed and reared. Mandy felt the straps tighten around her wrists and squinched her eyes shut, afraid that she was going to fall off. When the donkey thumped its front hooves on the ground, she bit her tongue and cried out in pain.

"Hey! Girly-girl awake!" The donkey jerked to a halt, and someone pulled her hair and yanked her head back.

"Let me go!" she screamed.

A squat, dirt-covered man stared at her with beady, black eyes. His straggly and matted hair was greasy and dirty, and his two front teeth were missing. He was wrapped head to foot in tarnished pieces of scrap metal, with a plate-like chest protector tied with frayed rope around his pudgy body.

"You're hurting me!" she screamed, again.

The man released his hold on her hair and Mandy's chin hit the donkey's side. What did he want with her? He stood grinning at her.

"Punquod! Hurry yourself up here!"

His foul breath assailed her and rough hands grabbed her arms and pulled her head first from the animal. Her captor flung her to the ground on her rear and then stood rocking from one foot to the other. Down the trail, another man was leading a shaggy donkey with Gwenydd strapped, stomach down, across its back. Mandy wondered if Gwenydd were hurt.

"Hurry, Punquod!"

Punquod arrived and giggled like a girl. Unlike her captor, Punquod was a bean pole, whose tattered pants stopped at the middle of his mud-caked calves. His toes, covered in grime, peeked out from torn sandals. Both men wore swords held by ropes tied around their middles, the squat man's sword short and stubby, the tall man's sword long and tapering.

Punquod unlashed Gwenydd and dumped her on the ground. She groaned. Mandy breathed a sigh of relief and scooted closer.

"Gwenydd," Mandy whispered. Gwenydd groaned again, and afraid that it might be a long time before she came to, Mandy shifted her body to examine the leather strips that bound her hands and feet. It would take a super sharp knife to cut them off. She rolled to sit up and see where they were.

Scrawny pine trees with roots that spread out in long runners clung to the sides of a sheer wall of craggy, red rock. Jagged boulders littered a rocky trail covered with pinecones and tufts of dry yellow grass. Straight in front of her across the trail, the rocky terrain ended in a cliff. While the sun shone straight down, heating the top of her head, Mandy watched Punquod tether the donkeys to a scraggly pine a few yards down the trail and the animals, scuffling and braying, tore at dried yellow grass sticking up through cracks in the rocks. The fat man gathered wood between Mandy and the cliff edge.

She continued to try to watch Gwenydd while a blackened kettle steamed above a triangle of burning pine logs. Mandy heard her stomach rumble and hoped that whatever was cooking would be edible.

The man stepped directly in front of her, grinning.

"Girly-girl hungry?"

"Get away from me!" she wailed.

He lunged forward, and she closed her eyes, fearing she had made him angry enough to hit her. She felt his hand hit her shoulder, and when she opened her eyes, she saw him drop a dead bee on the ground. *Did he save me from a bee sting,* Mandy wondered?

He laughed and Mandy, suddenly hurt and angry that he could laugh at them, two little kids.

"Untie us!"

"No," he said, "You'd just run away."

"Where are you taking us?" she asked.

"You're coming with me and Punquod. Right, Punquod?"

Punquod looked up, chewing with his mouth open, and said, "Yep, Gunta."

"We don't want to go with you." Mandy glared.

"Too bad," he answered. He caught a spider on his face and squashed it between his thumb and forefinger, then popped it into his mouth. Mandy looked away quickly, not wanting to think about what she had just seen. She hated these nasty men.

" I want to go home!" Mandy whined, on the verge of tears.

Punquod shook dead leaves, twigs, and bits of debris from his hair.

"I don't want girly-girls mad at me," he said, his mouth still crammed full. Gunta shuffled over to the fire and picked up a long handled spoon propped against a stone.

"They're just girly-girls, Punquod," Gunta said. "Harmless."

Gunta looked up from dipping the spoon into the kettle.

"If you girly-girls want to eat, tell me now 'fore I finish it all."

He plopped a nasty thick, dark green mass into a small bowl. Mandy did not think her stomach would keep it down. Gunta sat down and began to eat. Punquod put down his empty bowl and walked down the trail toward the donkeys.

Gwenydd groaned and Mandy turned toward her. The girl was struggling to sit up.

"Are you all right, Gwenydd?" Mandy whispered.

"My head hurts." Her freckles seemed dark on a face too white. "What has happened?"

"I think we have been kidnapped for ransom money," Mandy said softly.

"No!" Gwenydd gasped.

Mandy nodded.

"I think so, but I don't know for sure."

"What are we going to do?"

"I don't know."

Gwenydd scooted closer to Mandy.

"They are using fire, Mandy."

"So?"

"It's been forbidden by the priests of Belanos."

"Who's Belanos?"

"Belanos is Lord Dagda's and Lady Brighid's son. To keep us from harm, he forbids anyone to use fire."

Mandy remembered the meal Gwenydd had brought her at the Keep. The food had been cooked and hot.

"How do you cook, Gwenydd, if you don't use fire?"

"Faerlytes."

"What are faerlytes?"

"They're like the craerlytes, the blue crystals that made the light in your room. Faerlytes are red rocks that make heat to cook and keep warm with. The priests sell them at the church."

What a strange place this is, thought Mandy. *Does Father think it so strange?*

Mandy's stomach rumbled again.

"Do you have any bread?" she asked the strange men, loudly.

Gunta reached into a torn, bulky sack on the ground by the fire and pulled out a skinny loaf of crusty bread. He broke it into two pieces then tossed it on the dirt in front of the girls.

With hands tied, Mandy scooped up the bread and clumsily offered a piece to Gwenydd, and blew the dirt off her own piece. Hoping that the bread was edible, she began to ease it down.

"Gwenydd, we have to think of a way to get away," Mandy said between bites of bread.

"How can we, with our hands and feet tied?" Gwenydd asked.

"I don't know." If either Gunta or Punquod would put their sword down close by, then maybe she could cut the cords. The men seemed stupid, but were they that dumb?

Mandy stuck the last piece of dry bread into her mouth and watched Punquod checking the tethers on the donkeys. Satisfied, he scrambled back toward the cooking fire, where Gunta was plopping more nasty stuff into his bowl. Then as Gunta leaned forward to return the spoon to the kettle, Punquod stumbled into Gunta and Gunta knocked the kettle over into the fire. Punquod fell back hard on the sack with the bread, but Gunta fell forward with both hands into the burning firewood. He screamed as flame raced up his tattered shirt sleeve. Punquod struggled with gangling arms and legs to get up. Gunta jumped up and, hopping up and down, shook his burning sleeve.

"Put it out, put it out!" he shouted, but his movement fanned the fire up his shirt toward his elbow and then toward his shoulder.

"Stop! Drop! and Roll!" Mandy screamed. She had learned that way back in kindergarten with Miss Givens.

The burning sleeve now spread flame to the front of the shirt.

"Ahhhh," Gunta screamed flapping at the flames on his chest.

"Gunta," Mandy screamed again. "Stop!" He paused for a second, confused. "Drop in the dirt and roll!"

Gunta raised his burning arm to protect his face. Punquod, free from the sack, now stood looking with confusion at Mandy. He scooped and flung fist-fulls of dirt at Gunta.

"No, Punquod," Mandy rasped. "Get Gunta on the ground and then roll him in the dirt!"

Gunta never saw Punquod knock him to the ground, but within seconds, the flames were extinguished, and Mandy breathed a deep sigh. Only then did she realize that she had helped the enemy.

"Mandy, do you see?" Mandy looked at Gwenydd.

"Huh?"

"I told you that fire was forbidden, Mandy. Belanos gets angry when people do bad things, and he used Gunta's fire against him for bringing us here."

Punquod helped Gunta lean back against the sack, then turned to collect the black kettle and bowls that had scattered around the fire.

But, maybe now they would let them go. They must! It was only fair, she thought. "Punquod!" Mandy called, "Are you going to let us go now that I helped save Gunta's life?"

"Nope! Gunta and I gotta do what we planned to do."

Mandy had started feeling sorry for the creeps, but now anger at their unfairness in not letting them go flared within her. "Kidnapping kids?" she yelled.

Punquod looked hurt.

"We just sell slaves."

The white in Gwenydd's eyes almost made a circle around green irises.

"Slaves?" Mandy asked.

"Tradertown slaves?" Gwenydd asked.

"You got it, girly-girl," Gunta wheezed.

"What are Tradertown slaves?" Mandy asked.

"Anything their buyer wants 'em to be!" Punquod huffed.

Visions from movies, where slaves were beaten and abused, flashed through Mandy's mind. She would die if subjected to treatment like that. She would get away, she thought suddenly, she would! She wished she had a knife so she could slice through the cords and make her escape.

Punquod picked up the sack stuffed with the black kettle and bowls, secured it to a donkey, then untethered the animals and walked them up the trail to the girls.

"Stand up, girly-girls. It's time to get moving."

Mandy stomped on her feet. She felt dirty and terrible and didn't want to be flung across the animal's back like a bag of feed again. "Can't we ride sitting up?" she asked.

Punquod rubbed his chin with his dirty hands. "Don't see why not as long as you stay there."

He picked her up and sat her side-saddle on the donkey, then took his knife and cut the cords that bound her ankles together. When she moved her left leg across the donkey's back, Punquod reached under the donkey to retie the cord drawing it tight around both legs.

Punquod settled Gwenydd on the other donkey and then pointed both animals up the trail. The sun, now on the horizon to Mandy's right, shone from a blue, pink, and yellow-orange sky that merged with the violet-blue sparkling water. If she could escape, then she would have to get her bearings. Mandy remembered when she had been on a Girl Scout hike and the leader had told her how. *Let me see,* thought Mandy, *the sun is setting on my right. That would be west. We must be moving south, then. To get back to the Keep I'll have to travel north. Remember that.* She turned her attention back to the trail. She would keep as many landmarks in her mind as possible.

With every step, Gunta groaned and complained, his arm in a makeshift sling, while Punquod followed, singing off key. Before long, they were traveling through dark shadows up a deep red chasm into mountains, sunlight fading fast.

CHAPTER EIGHTEEN

BEHOLD THE POWERS OF SPIRIT
JOIN THE CIRCLE OF BLUE.

Standing between Wren and Serhonydd high up on the slope, Katherine looked toward Wry's Ken. Where the town touched the sea, sailboats, painted red, purple, yellow, and green with matching spinnakers, skimmed across choppy water. The glossy boat colors contrasted with the town's white buildings and red peaked roofs. Above the roofs near the center of town, she saw a huge blue-domed building with four blue minarets sparkling like sea water in the morning sun.

"What's that blue building?" she asked. Serhonydd seemed preoccupied with his thoughts, but Wren answered. "That's the Holy Hall where the Blue Sorcerers live."

It looks like a mosque, she thought. "Is that where we're going?" she asked.

"Yes," Wren answered.

That evening, when Katherine followed Serhonydd through an arched gate in a southern wall of Wry's Ken, she saw a cobblestone street that twisted past sharp-cornered two-storied buildings. Walking under a brightly painted wooden sign outside a dress shop, she peered up at another sign that sported a gold and green feather stuck in a mug filled with suds. "The Parrot's Nest," Wren said, as sounds of men laughing erupted from its dusky interior and Katherine guessed it housed a tavern. When she slowed down to gape at a red-fringed skirt in a dingy glass window, Wren tugged her arm.

Past a butcher shop, she gazed into a window where rubies, emeralds, and diamonds littered a drop cloth at the bottom of a box with gold and silver chains draped across its open lid. The jewels might not have been real, she thought, but the dagger displayed in the leather belt at the jeweler's waist was very real steel. Farther down the street, a juggler in green and purple leather skipped nimbly along the street, clicking large glass marbles in the air. Dark-haired men in leather britches and tunics, and dark-eyed women in long flowing gowns hurried past Katherine. A shop owner, sweeping dirt into the street, noticed Katherine staring at him and turned quickly away.

His black robes a-swirl, Serhonydd strode relentlessly through the twisting streets. High above his head and the red-tiled roofs, one of the tall ice-blue minarets shimmered like a film of water on a field of snow in moonlight. Serhonydd stopped and turned back, regarding her with a scowl. Since crossing the waterfall, he had been acting more and more strangely. Maybe he didn't want to help her. Maybe she was stupid to trust him, and he was leading her into trouble. She looked at his stony face and sighed. Still, it had felt good to have him help her, and either Wry was some ultimate plot concocted by who knows whom to drive her crazy, or Wry was real and Serhonydd sincere. With a sharp twist of boot against cobblestone, he turned and strode toward the center of the town where the minarets rose into a pink backdrop of sunset. Trying to find out what was bothering this strange man would have to wait.

By the time they arrived at the gate of the blue mosque, the cobblestone street was dark with long shadows. The gate swung back, and a short, stocky man in a dark habit motioned them in. Once they were inside, she found herself standing under a colonnade of shimmering blue stone that tunneled beneath dark leaved trees. At the far end, blue-white light twinkled from windows and archways of a massive building that jutted into a starry sky. Their steps echoing into the night, the man guided them along a stone path under the colonnade to a corner where from windows of a blue stone minaret as large as a barn silo at home, Katherine saw blue light splash across the path. Opening a door in the side of the minaret, the man led them into an eight-sided room where blue light poured from craerlytes set like torches around its walls. The most striking feature of the empty room was a spiral staircase of stone that rose at least thirty feet and disappeared into the ceiling above. When prodded by Wren, Katherine moved to follow the man and Serhonydd up the stairs. By the time she had circled the spiral twice, her vertigo made her keep her eyes glued to the steps directly in front of her. She did not want to look down.

At the top of the stairs, Katherine stepped into a room with floor-to-ceiling arched windows set into each of the room's eight sides. In the middle of the room, separated by a small marble table, two fur-covered couches faced each other. Their guide disappeared down the stairs, and Serhonydd sprawled on one of the couches. Katherine walked over to sit opposite Serhonydd on the low couch, and Shaeff flopped at her feet. Serhonydd's face, darkly shadowed with stubble, looked out an arched window where Wren stood peering over a balcony. Serhonydd's jaw seemed set to receive bad news. Whoever they were meeting, she thought, must be important.

Serhonydd's stormy eyes met hers and, blushing at being caught observing him, she looked away. She hoped that he could not read her mind like Shaeff.

"*Hmm?*" Shaeff looked up from his position at her feet, his ears notched forward in a listening position.

Nothing, she thought and reached down to scratch him behind the ears. He sighed and put his head down on his paws.

Serhonydd rose awkwardly and Katherine, not sure what to do, did the same. From the stairs stepped a small woman with silver hair falling across her shoulders. She stood in a gown of shimmering blue and stared at Serhonydd. She then turned to look at Katherine, bowed gracefully, and suddenly smiled. Faint crow's feet creased the corners of the most beautiful violet eyes Katherine had ever seen. Her face was smooth and glowed with health. Behind the woman, a tall slim man in a shimmering white-and-blue corded tunic over pants tucked into blue boots bowed slightly, then raised his eyes to look kindly at Katherine. His black hair and short-cropped beard were streaked with silver. Serhonydd sat down, and Wren stepped into the room from the balcony. Katherine felt uncomfortable. Why were these people bowing to her?

"Katherine?" the woman asked, her voice soft and melodious.

"You know my name?" Katherine asked.

"I know many things," the woman said, gesturing with her hand as if it were not important. "I am called Lady A'legra, and this," she pointed to the man who had entered the room behind her, "is my spirit bondsman, Lord A'leron." He smiled gently, nodded politely, and sat next to Serhonydd on the couch. Shaeff padded over to the older man, and within seconds the telepack was sighing contentedly as Lord A'leron rubbed his ear. Watching him with the dog, Katherine decided that Lord A'leron's mouth and eyes were an older version of Serhonydd's. She wondered if they were related.

Now the woman gestured for Katherine to sit and strangely, not knowing why, Katherine offered her hand and the lady's long-fingered hand covered her own in a warm grasp. She did not understand why she felt glad to meet this woman, but she did. The woman, appearing confident and totally relaxed, sat back on the couch and drew Katherine down beside her. Serhonydd gripped his hands together until the knuckles turned white. Wren leaned against the window frame.

"Now, Katherine," Lady A'legra said, gently patting Katherine's hand. "We have much to discuss."

Serhonydd's cold blue eyes fixed on her, but Katherine could read nothing in their depths. If this woman knew her name, did that mean she knew where Mandy was, too?

"I am a Blue Sorcerer, Katherine," Lady A'legra said. "For many years, the rune stones have foretold that a Seeker will come to Wry to find that which is a part of her. The Seeker is to come wearing the Band of Brocoudahl and holding Flame in her hands. The rune stones revealed that she would need my help. But she would be linked to the Dark Imperator." She raised one eyebrow and peered closely at Katherine. "Now you arrive at the Holy Hall wearing the Band of Brocoudahl."

Katherine reached up to touch the Band. "That's what Wren called it."

Lady A'legra nodded. "And, you hold the Flame."

"My Dad's lighter?" Katherine laughed. She had never heard anything so ludicrous.

"And," Lady A'legra spoke softly, "you need help in finding your daughter." Katherine could feel the pressure of Lady A'legra's hand on hers. "Yes," Katherine said, "I have looked by myself without finding her."

Lady A'legra said quietly, "Tell us how you came here."

As Katherine told them her story, the frustration of not finding Mandy grew into an ache in her heart. To hold back the tears, she took a deep breath, and then she told them about following the blue flame, falling into the water in the pond, and finding the key. A look passed from Lady A'legra to Lord A'leron, a look that somehow seemed to share forbidden knowledge. "What key, Katherine?" Lord A'leron asked, sitting forward.

She reached under her blouse to pull out the pouch, extracted the key, a narrow shaft with a flat end filigreed with entwined circles, then handed it to Lord A'leron. He carefully examined it, turning it over in his hand, and handed it to Lady A'legra, who studied it. "It is the Key of K'vle," she said, handing it back. Katherine dropped it back into the pouch.

"If the legends are true," Lady A'legra said, "it will unlock the Jeweled Locket around the neck of the One-Horne."

"Is that important?" she asked.

Lady A'legra turned to Lord A'leron. "You are more familiar with the legends than I," Lady A'legra said to him. "Explain it to her."

"Understand, Katherine," Lord A'leron said, "that what I say is based on what Dru'dammen legends have said will come to pass. The fact that you are here adds veracity to these legends, and I suppose as time reveals more, we Blue Sorcerers will understand more. But the legends say that Lord Dagda and Lady Brighid put something into the Locket then commanded the One-Horne to carry and keep it away from human hands. Whatever the gods put inside the Locket was held there with only the Key of K'vle to release it."

"And now I have that key," said Katherine softly.

"So it would seem," replied Lord A'leron.

Katherine thought she was doing well to keep track of all the information that Lord A'leron was telling her.

"But, what does all of this have to do with Mandy?" she asked.

Lady A'legra patted Katherine's hand.

"Kylasar," Lord A'leron said, "needs to find and capture the One-Horne. According to legend, the One-Horne will only come to a child of innocence and Kylasar's daughter."

"If I find Mandy and take her back to Earth before he finds the One-Horne, then he will not be able to get the Locket."

"Correct." Lord A'leron smiled as he sat back against the couch.

"But, why does Kylasar want what is in the Locket?" Katherine asked.

"What is in the Locket. I surmise, however, that whatever is in the Locket will give Kylasar more power to do his evil deeds. If you find your daughter and take her home, then Kylasar will not be able to take from the One-Horne the contents of the Jeweled Locket. And Kylasar will not obtain the power to destroy Wry."

"But, I don't even know whether or not she is on Wry!" Katherine said.

Serhonydd stood. "Why not ask Lady A'legra and Lord A'leron to help you, Katherine? After all, they are Blue Sorcerers."

Lady A'legra and Lord A'leron turned to Serhonydd. The room suddenly grew chill. Katherine watched Serhonydd's eyes challenge them. Lady A'legra frowned, her eyes like cold amethysts fixed on Serhonydd's face. Then softly she sighed. "If you are not willing to use your power to help Katherine, then should she not ask our help?"

Katherine did not know what power Lady A'legra was talking about. "But, he has helped me," she said.

Lady A'legra shook her head, her long hair shimmering. Evidently, this conversation was hers and Serhonydd's. "He has brought you here, true, but he could have helped you without our help. However, he disregards his own destiny and shirks the Power."

Serhonydd's face darkened. "I saw the deaths it led to."

"But the Power is your heritage," Lord A'leron firmly stated, "and you should not turn away from it."

"I have turned away from it!" Serhonydd said through clenched teeth. He strode from the room. Lady A'legra heaved another sigh. Lord A'leron peered closely into Katherine's eyes and, evidently satisfied with what he found there, nodded. "Yes, Serhonydd is our son, the only mage in this generation conceived of two spirit-bonded Blue Sorcerers. As such, he has the potential for tapping untold power, power that crisscrosses Wry to create life." He looked sadly at Lady A'legra. "Yet, he refuses to take and use this power."

"Why does he refuse?" Katherine asked.

Lord A'leron looked grim. "When Serhonydd was a child, Kylasar's troops destroyed a Yttoshamen village. When Lady A'legra and I found the tortured and mutilated bodies of the men, women, and children, we were so enraged that we used our power to eradicate the soldiers. In our anger, we sank to their vileness. Instead of confronting us with our corruption of power, Serhonydd blamed the power for corrupting us." He looked down. "And now he refuses the power for fear that it will corrupt him."

"And can this power you speak of bring Mandy here?"

"Patience, Katherine," Lady A'legra said. She stood up, seemingly to end the discussion. Lady A'legra offered her hand to Lord A'leron, who rose. He said, "We need to consult the *ys yw wedydd*. In the meantime, we will see to it that you and Wren are made comfortable."

Wait! Katherine wanted to say. *I must find Mandy now!* She looked at Wren. He shrugged his shoulders but looked resigned. With a heavy heart, Katherine watched the sorcerers leave the room. She stood up, walked past Wren where he still stood against the window frame to the balcony, and looked out into the twilight. Far below, the lights from the town twinkled. A cool breeze brushed against her face, and she breathed deeply, smelling meat cooking and bread baking. Off in the distance, she heard laughter and shouts from people hurrying home. *I won't cry,* she thought and took another deep breath.

She looked up to see stars lighting the cloudless sky and thought how each star by itself sparked a light that when added to the light from other stars, banished the dark from the night sky.

Maybe, she prayed, the Blue Sorcerers would find a way to help her.

CHAPTER NINETEEN

O WAYWARD SON, YOUR ANGER FLARES OR IS IT BUT FALSE PRIDE?

After he left Katherine and Wren, Serhonydd could still feel his parents' anger. He had known it would come to this, but Katherine had had to talk to Lady A'legra. He was distraught, he decided, otherwise why would he be heading for his mentor's chambers? Portemas, dead for ten years now, had once taught Serhonydd of the True Path, the path of enlightenment, the way of nonviolence. Serhonydd himself, not wanting anyone to desecrate or destroy Portemas' diaries and writings on his revelations about the True Path, had sealed the chamber with a warding spell, thinking to return one day after his hermitage and take up his mentor's work. But, the years had passed and … well, the years had passed.

At the door to Portemas' chamber, Serhonydd hesitated. Was his warding spell still working? He cleared his mind to receive the runes magically drawn by him in the air years ago. Their intricate lines began glowing faintly on the wooden door. Any Blue Sorcerer could have seen the runes and broken the ward, but the runes were still intact. *By his mother's command?* he wondered and thanked whatever gods had left Portemas' world untouched. He raised his hand and erased the lines joining the runes. His ears popped as if there had been a change in air pressure, and the door swung inward. The gloom of the room settled about him like a well-worn cloak. Here was the only real home Serhonydd had ever known.

He reached out his hand and felt the reassuring touch of the craerlyte in its niche beside the door, and without thinking, he produced the hum deep inside his throat. The musical vibration passed along his arm and down his fingers, and the familiar blue light glowed.

The room was as it had been at the time of Portemas' death, but every surface was thick with dust. Volumes and parchments on philosophy, literature, and religion were still strewn the desk by the window. A small bed, with its covers crumpled, stood against one wall. Bookcases lined the other three. Remembering the months he had agonized over those books crammed with ideas too deep for a young boy's normal thoughts, Serhonydd sighed. He sat down on the bed. Now he remembered the bright flush on Katherine's cheeks when he had stormed out of the tower room. Had he embarrassed her? Had he made a complete and utter fool of himself? Probably, but what did that matter? Why was it so important that he make a good impression on her? He pictured her green eyes flashing angrily at him when she had asked what was wrong. He was a grown man, long past his youth. How could he tell her that he was afraid to talk to his parents?

The past few days had seemed unbearable while he watched her with Wren, who thrived on all the attention she gave him. When Katherine had leaned against Wren after crossing the waterfall, Serhonydd had wanted to take her hand, to touch her, to listen to her tell him about herself. His heart seemed to ache with strange feelings that he had never felt before. Was this what it felt like to find a spirit bondsman? Had his father ever felt like this? He felt responsible for Katherine's well-being and would follow wherever her quest sent them.

Her quest—Serhonydd shook his head. He had wanted to keep his promise to Portemas to never use the power for destructive purposes. Never before had he questioned Portemas' teachings, yet he felt them wrong now. There was no justification in promoting nonviolence while Kylasar schemed to destroy the Yttomshamen and Wry. Serhonydd would have to take up the power and destroy the Imperator. But what if it were too late to take the power?

Serhonydd stood. *Perhaps,* he thought, *Katherine and the Band of Brocoudahl would suffice and eliminate Kylasar.* Then he would not have to find out that he had been wrong all these years.

CHAPTER TWENTY

EARTH POWERS IN WANDERER'S WAND POINT TO THE SEEKER'S CHILDE.

Katherine was wiping the sugar off the last pastry from her fingers when Lady A'legra and Lord A'leron stepped into the room. Lady A'legra carried a wooden staff almost as tall as she was. She held it out to Katherine. At the top was embedded a crystal as big as a robin's egg and along the delicately carved shaft, ivy curled and trailed among embossed animals and rune-like characters. If she looked forever, Katherine thought, she wouldn't see all that its surface contained. "Are you giving me this?" Katherine wondered out loud.

Lady A'legra nodded. "It will help you."

Katherine was startled to feel the wood's shape change in her hand to fit her grip perfectly. "What is it?" she asked.

"It is a Wanderer's Wand. Now," Lady A'legra said, "call your daughter's name, Katherine, out loud or silently."

Katherine, not sure what would happen, called softly, "Mandy!" Immediately, deep within the crystal, a clear white light gleamed dimly and disappeared. Katherine raised her eyes to Lady A'legra.

"Call her again," Lady A'legra said, "and this time, hold the Wand in front of you and turn until you see the spark brighten."

"Mandy!" Katherine called again, pivoting slowly on the balls of her feet. The Wanderer's Wand flickered briefly, then blinked out. Katherine stopped her pivot, moved back to the position where she had been when the light came on and turned in the opposite direction. The white light pulsated, throwing bits of rainbows across the floor, walls, and furniture in the room, and then steadily brightened until Katherine had to turn her eyes away. "What does it mean?" Katherine whispered.

"It means you will always know which direction to go to find your daughter."

"How far away is she?" Katherine asked.

"There is no way to know for sure, Katherine," Lord A'leron said. "She could be minutes or weeks away, but you will be heading in the right direction." *Not like before,* Katherine thought, *when I checked every bus and railroad station in Akron.* Remembering all the dead ends, Katherine felt a lump at the back of her throat. "Well, what are we waiting for?" she asked. "Let's go find her!"

"You will have to search for her without us, Katherine," Lord A'leron said. "The *ys yw wedydd* say that the battle for Wry is fought Kylasar to Kylasar, and that none may interfere."

"What do you mean?" Katherine sat down, confused. "Do you expect me to actually physically fight Eric?" She could hear hysteria in her voice. "I hate fighting! I will not fight Eric … or Kylasar. I only want to find Mandy and go home. Nothing more."

"Do you not see, Katherine," Lady A'legra said urgently, "Kylasar will not willingly let Mandy go. It is your destiny in seeking your daughter to fight Kylasar for her release. If you win her back, Wry will survive, but if you fail, Kylasar and his evil will destroy Wry."

"How will I fight him?" Katherine demanded. "With a sword? With my fists?" She heard the desperation in her voice. "I don't know how to fight!"

"You will fight him, Katherine. It has been foretold. But, understand this," Lord A'leron said. "By whatever means you are fated to fight him, you will have the Power to do so. That, too, has been foretold."

It was not fair, Katherine decided, that she was expected to solve Wry's problems with Kylasar. All she wanted to do was to find Mandy and take her home. If she could do that without Eric knowing, all the better. "I will protect Mandy and myself the best I can from Eric, and if possible, I'll take Mandy away without him knowing we've gone."

"You can only do as you think right," Lord A'leron said. "In the morning, you will be given supplies to continue your search."

Next day, the crisp morning air whipped the smell of salt from the sea. Wren whistled for Shaeff, who came at a trot, his long tail fanning out like a flag behind him. With Wry's Ken behind them, their packs filled with provisions, and the Wanderer's Wand in her hand, Katherine and Wren walked toward the western horizon swollen with the scraggy, Black Ridge Mountains. Serhonydd had elected to stay behind. Not understanding why, Katherine thought perhaps it was for the best. She had grown tired of his attitude.

Up ahead, periwinkle blue-and-silver-leaved trees dotted the landscape. Katherine looked for the golden seagulls that had graced the skies along the trail to Wry's Ken, but saw instead birds with iridescent burgundy and gold feathers swirling and flashing in and out of occasional bushes along the way. Yellow butterflies as big as her hand fluttered over clumps of red, blue, and yellow wildflowers. Shaeff snapped at a butterfly and when he missed, Katherine laughed.

"You're so funny, Shaeff," she thought, patting his head.

"I was only having a bit of sport."

"But what if you'd caught that butterfly?"

"No chance of that," he snorted. *"It was too fast."*

Now before them was a series of jagged rocky outcroppings and sparse grass ascending to an almost vertical cliff face of reddish-orange rock. Katherine followed Wren up a steep and rocky ridge. The sun grew hot and the cool sea breeze dissipated.

Sweat slid down Katherine's neck, and her shirt clung to her back. She watched Wren use his walking stick and at first thought it a sacrilege to use the Wand in the same way. But the trail became steeper, and soon she was digging the Wand into the dirt and pulling herself forward with it.

The sun was directly overhead when they came to the base of the cliff, its surface marred with jutting rock and deep fissures.

"Now where?" she asked Wren.

"Up."

"It doesn't look easy," she said apprehensively. She doubted that she could climb the cliff.

"It's not too bad," Wren said, grinning. "Just do not look down." Moving behind her, he threaded the Wand through her pack. "You will need your hands free, Katherine." Wren then turned to the cliff face. Finding crevices, nooks, and thick rooted plants to pull up on, he reached with a hand or raised his foot and shifted his weight and ascended.

Katherine was dismayed. "I can't do it," she called.

Above her, Wren never slowed, his fingers grabbing jutting rock, his feet kicking loose rock down the almost vertical face. "Watch out below and come on!" he shouted over his shoulder.

"Hurry up, Katherine!" Startled, she looked up to see Shaeff far up the cliff. Fearing she would surely fall and break her neck, Katherine cautiously stretched her arms above her head and slid her fingers across the jagged rocks protruding from the cliff. She held her head back to see what she was doing, quickly earned a tired neck, and learned to find a hand hold by feel alone. Then she lowered her head and looked at her feet. With the top of her head against the rock, she found a small crevice and inserted her right foot. She pulled up with her hands and pushed with her right foot. When she couldn't find a place for her left foot, she nearly panicked. Then her left foot connected with solid rock and she paused, breathing hard. The strain on her arms grew painful, but she stretched one arm higher and felt for a new handhold, moved her other hand to a new hold, eased one foot up to a new position, then followed with her other foot. Her body protested, muscles knotting and tensing, the pack straps biting into her shoulders, but finally she reached the top of the cliff. *I made it!* she thought. Dusting dirt from her hands, she turned to look over the ledge. Beneath her, Wry's Ken was only a splattering of color against the cobalt backdrop of sea. Her head spinning from vertigo, she sat down. Then she saw that the cliff was only the first of many that continued jaggedly upward. Wren smiled. "Just take one cliff at a time, Katherine."

"Before I take another step, I want to rest."

Standing on the rocks above, Shaeff telesent, *"We should go. You can rest later."*

Soon Katherine's world became nothing more than a sweaty struggle to climb the red-orange rock with the hot yellow sun beating down upon her back. Her hands grabbed at scrub and small saplings in cracks filled with bits of dark red soil. Her hands felt like they had been scraped raw and she was bruised all over.

Finally, beneath an overhang that hid them from the sun, they rested. Katherine slipped her pack from her shoulders. The loss of its weight was sheer joy, and the journey cakes and dried fruit were a feast. The shadows cooled her. "Are we done traveling for the day?" she asked.

"There are at least four more hours of sun left in the day, and we need to take advantage of it," Wren said.

She groaned. "How come you don't seem to mind all this climbing?" she asked.

"I do it all the time," he replied. He took a swallow of nightroot, then handed Katherine the bottleskin. "The night Shaeff and I found you, we had been scouting the Fogfiend Mountains for enemies. If the Guardians had been slacking in their duty, Kylasar, your Eric, would have destroyed Crystal Caer a long time ago."

What else would Eric destroy, she wondered. *Was Mandy in physical danger? Eric had never hurt the girl before, but would he hurt her, now?* She felt anger rise within her, and she knew in that moment, that if Eric—or Kylasar—hurt Mandy, she would kill him. The thought shocked her.

"We need to go," Wren said.

Katherine sighed.

CHAPTER TWENTY-ONE

O WAYWARD SON, THE SEEKER'S FATE DEPENDS ON JARYDD'S KNOWLEDGE.

From a dark doorway, Serhonydd had watched Katherine, Wren, and Shaeff leave Wry's Ken. Later, he would find them, but first, he had to learn as much as he could about the battle of Kylasar and Kylasar. He turned toward the Archives.

At the stone archway, wide stone steps slippery with moss spiraled down toward underground vaults. Serhonydd trailed his hand along huge blocks of a stone wall wondering at the mason's skill in creating such a perfect joining of thick rock. When he stepped onto a landing, he turned to enter a doorway that led to the Archives.

Once inside, Serhonydd felt the same awe that he had felt here as a small boy. The walls, the foundation of the Holy Hall above, were of the same thick stone that lined the stairwell. At the center of the room, four black marble pillars arched into a vaulted ceiling with two pillars along each wall. Inset in holders head high on the pillars were craerlytes, their blue-tinged light illuminating massive bookshelves overflowing with thousands of books. Just under the central archway and straight in front of Serhonydd, at a massive oak table covered with piles of books sat the Archivist, his stocky form like that of a toad, hunched over a dusty volume. Serhonydd spoke quietly. "Hello, Jarydd."

Jarydd looked up from his book. Under a balding head covered with tufts of white fuzzy hair, his smooth moon face turned toward the shadow. "Who's there?"

Ten years was a long time, and Serhonydd knew that the Archivist might fail to recognize him. Serhonydd walked forward and stopped in front of the table. "Serhonydd."

Jarydd grinned. He dusted his chubby white hands together, the fingers stained purple from ink and propped his elbows on the parchment. The sleeves of his robe dropped to expose flabby forearms mottled with more ink stains. "What can I do for you, my boy!" he asked, his voice cracking with a slight vibrato.

Serhonydd remembered the frustration he had felt as a boy when trying to elicit answers from Jarydd's long, seemingly empty soliloquies. He crossed his arms and looked at the shelves and books stacked on top of each other. The books in Jarydd's domain were like weeds left to run amok in a garden. Serhonydd carefully posed his question. "Where might I find information on the Imperator Kylasar?"

Jarydd's pleasant grin dropped immediately into a look of consternation. "I, ah ... have many volumes on the Imperator."

Jarydd was not going to make it easy on him. "Well, then," Serhonydd said, "let us begin with a small, exact history of the man."

"Oh," Jarydd said. He hurried off into the stacks to return with a small green, well-worn book. "This is Balsak's *Histories of Personified Evils*. You may not know that Balsak was once Kylasar's apprentice and, although some maintain that the book is extremely biased, most agree that Balsak came as close as possible to telling the truth." He stood beaming up at Serhonydd. "Now, what else?"

"I will need a volume that tells about the legends of Kylasar versus Kylasar."

"Worlds' End!" Jarydd whispered, his eyes round, lids rapidly blinking. "What all the legends foretell that when Kylasar meets Kylasar, the world as we know it ends!"

"I seriously doubt that."

"Well, it's in the Text of Belanos, and the Yttoshamen swear by it."

Serhonydd's patience was beginning to wear thin. "Do you have a text?"

"Of course!" Jarydd disappeared once again into the stacks and returned with three large texts cradled in his arms. Serhonydd groaned. He did not have the time to read them all. Jarydd dumped them on top of the book spread open on the table. "There now! This should keep you busy for a while." He looked pleased with himself.

"Just give me the one with the most information. I'll return for the others later, if I have the time."

Jarydd offered him a plain brown book. "This is the one that Lady A'legra and Lord A'leron look in for their answers."

Serhonydd took the book and walked away. At the doorway, he turned back to thank Jarydd, but the little man was already immersed in his book.

CHAPTER TWENTY-TWO

THE CIRCLE OF BLUE SENDS MAGIC TO SOFTEN THE SEEKER'S PATH.

The sun had already set and the air had grown chilly, when farther up the mountain in a small cave, Katherine took her cloak from her pack and wrapped it around her shoulders. She could understand now why Wren had wanted to find shelter before dark. Time and again, her feet had dislodged loose stones over the side. She had heard them bounce against the rocks below and had no trouble imagining herself slipping off, bouncing like the stones down onto the jagged rocks.

Wren lit the craerlyte and from his pack tossed her a roll of material, no thicker than a piece of cardboard. "Your bedroll," he explained.

"There's no way I can sleep on that! I'll feel every rock and pebble."

Wren snapped the bedroll out to its full length on the floor of the cave. "Lie down on it, Katherine," he ordered.

She lay on top of the material. Feeling the rock hardness against her hips and shoulder blades, she glared up at him.

"Close your eyes," Wren said.

Immediately after she closed her eyes, she felt an odd stirring in the cloth. She squirmed and felt undulations lapping against her body as if she were floating on water. She opened her eyes and the ground solidified under her and some protuberance jabbed her kidney. She closed her eyes again and instantly returned to the magic "water bed." Wren stood over her, grinning.

"How?" She sputtered.

"Just thank the Blue Sorcerers."

"Did they give us anything else magical?"

"Not that I know of," Wren answered.

CHAPTER TWENTY-THREE

POWERS OF WATER HIDE THE SEEKER BEHIND A MAGIC CURTAIN.

By the third night in the mountains, Katherine felt like an exhausted composite of dirt and tired muscles. She was clumsy and fearful. Only that day, she had stood too petrified to move her foot across a crevasse. But Wren had sensed her fear and diverted her morbid thoughts into laughter.

Now they were camped thousands of feet high, under an orange slab of jagged stone. Katherine shivering, gazed down along the western side of the mountains where the last rays of setting sun painted shadows of vermilion deepening in the crevices to purple. Earlier, Wren had pointed far beyond the sharp rocks to a river, the Red River, wider and calmer than the Ridge River, curling through a yellow grassy plain that stretched into an orange smear near the horizon.

Then she noticed a black dot swiftly moving against the horizon toward the mountain. It was much too big for a bird.

Katherine felt the Band of Brocoudahl grow warm, and suddenly with her new inner vision she saw against the last rays of light a fast-approaching darkness glide toward them. Glowing red eyes raked the mountainside.

"Rathrider!" Katherine hissed into the silence.

"Hide!" Shaeff urged, nudging her back from the precipice. *"Get the gear inside!"*

Hurrying under the dark overhang, Wren snatched up both packs, but Katherine stood confused.

"Hurry!" Wren yelled, and pulled her under the overhang. Shaeff, already there, sat on his haunches and growled deeply. Heart pounding, Katherine clutched at Wren's sleeve, and together they pressed their backs against the rock wall.

"Do not move," Shaeff said in her mind. Katherine tried to hold her breath, then watched in horror as the winged apparition flew toward them. She tried to push herself into the rock at her back, the overhang creating the illusion of a cavern.

At an unholy, piercing scream, Katherine felt the hair rise on the back of her neck. Then a huge bat with needle-sharp teeth and long pointed ears dropped its talons on the ledge in front of the overhang. Katherine covered her nose and mouth to avoid the stench. On the bat creature's back rode a being with glaring red eyes that, like an inky blot, flowed, pooled on the ground then elongated into a thin, shimmering shadow man, who stood and slowly swept its red glowing eyes toward the overhang.

Katherine pressed against the rock, struggling to stay quiet, her throat clamped down on a scream she felt building deep inside. The red eyes grew brighter, and she closed her own in fear and wished that she were behind an impenetrable wall.

With that thought, the Band of Brocoudahl grew uncomfortably hot, and a spark of blue flame crackled, hit the floor slithering like a liquid snake across the rock, split with two blue lines of light heading toward each wall under the overhang, and then shimmied up the walls across the ceiling to join in the middle. Once the ends connected, the blue-white light across the ceiling dropped a thin, translucent blue-light curtain between Katherine and the Rathrider. She stared, amazed.

Surely, she thought, the Rathrider could still see them crouched behind the curtain of light, but its red eyes moved away from the overhang searching the mountain above.

The bat-creature screamed until the Rathrider flowed up the reptilian leg, poured into the saddle, and jerked the reins hard. The bat-creature shrieked, kicking loose dirt and shale, and leapt from the edge of the escarpment and, with giant leathery black wings blotting out chunks of sky, swept into the star-studded night. Katherine exhaled slowly and inhaled, fresh smelling air. The stench was gone. She reached toward the blue-white curtain, which cascaded down around her, drifting away from the rock. Quick as lightning, a blue radiance rimmed her fingertips, tickled her skin raising the hair down the length of her arms, and then flickered out.

"What was it?" Wren asked.

Katherine rubbed her arms trying to rid her skin of goose bumps.

"I don't know, but whatever it was, it kept us hidden from that … thing!"

"I wonder if you can do it again," Wren said.

"You think I did it?" Katherine asked.

Wren pointed to the Band.

"Just before the light materialized, the Band sparked. Did you not sense it?"

Closing her eyes, Katherine thought back to wishing to be invisible or to have a wall to hide behind. She did not feel magical but wished for a curtain, a blue magic wall to hide behind. She opened one eye and looked around: nothing. She shut the eye and wished again, harder. The band stayed cool against her forehead. Opening both eyes, she saw disappointment on Wren's face.

"I guess you are not able to do it at will," he sighed and reached for his pack.

"Do you think Kylasar knows I'm on Wry?" she asked.

"Why else send the Rathrider after you?"

"Wren," she mused, "if the Wand keeps pointing west, then there won't be any place to hide once we are on the plains."

"You cannot tell from here, but the plains grasses are taller than our heads. Your Band appears to give you ample warning when the Rathrider approaches, and if we are lucky, the People of the Plains might help hide us."

"People of the Plains? Who are they?"

"Friends of mine." Wren sipped at the Nightroot and then recorked the bottle. "Perhaps their shaman, Totatis, could give us more information on Kylasar." Wren handed the bottle to Katherine.

"I don't want to waste time, Wren," Katherine pleaded.

"We'll see. The People are so elusive, we might not find them even if we wanted to."

Long into the night, Katherine lay, eyes fixed on the stars blinking outside the overhang. While her back ached from the rough ground, she prayed that Eric cared enough for Mandy to keep her safe.

CHAPTER TWENTY-FOUR

BEHOLD -- THE POWERS OF SPIRIT
HELP THE SEEKER GROW.

Two days had passed and no Rathrider had appeared. Still, Katherine knew that if Eric had sent it, the Rathrider would be back. Eric never gave up. Bone weary, scratched, and covered with dust, but glad that she no longer needed as much rest as when they first started up the mountain, Katherine descended a rocky path on the western slope of the Black Ridge Mountains. She gazed westward across the yellow plain to the bright ribbon of Red River. The plain stretched west before her with no breeze stirring its grass. With the sky turning a brilliant, cloudless blue, the day would become hot.

At the base of the mountain, Katherine followed Wren into a resilient curtain of yellow grass. Gnats flitted around her eyes, mouth, and nose. Katherine raised the Wand to drive them away, but they regrouped and swarmed closer. As the morning passed, fine yellow pollen from flower clusters like corn tassels thickly powdered the air until she was walking through a yellow haze. Her nose tickled with pollen, and she sneezed. Her mouth tasted like she had eaten dandelion petals. Her neck and shoulders ached from the weight of the backpack.

"Wren," she called, "can we stop?"

"In a bit," he said over his shoulder.

He did not seem to care how uncomfortable she was. In irritation, she paused to shift her pack and then Wren was gone in the yellow haze of tall grass.

"Wren!" she called.

"What?"

His voice sounded close and hearing him in the grass behind her, she turned. Katherine gasped. Peering through the haze behind stalks of grass was a pair of large brown eyes in a pale oval face. Then another face popped into view, and another and then, another. Backing up, she held the Wand in front of her.

"Wren!" she whispered loudly.

Wren thrashed through the grass behind her and stopped at her side.

"What's wrong?"

A yellow-skinned creature three feet tall stepped through the grass and moved gracefully toward her.

"A child!" she said, and Wren started to laugh.

"No," he replied, "Terlooeth Teig."

The childlike creature's long cornsilk hair flowed to its ankles. A yellow body suit like a second skin hugged its small form. Now Katherine could see that this creature was no child, but a woman perfectly proportioned for her height, an athletic, sleek feline in motion, who stopped without a sound, perfectly poised on the balls of her bare feet, apparently ready to bolt if need be. Then two other women and three men slipped behind the first woman, all with the same sculptured faces, delicate noses, and bow-shaped mouths. Although they all resembled each other, none had the long tresses the woman in front of Katherine had. All moved gracefully and quietly, and blended almost perfectly into their surroundings. *That is why I could only see their eyes in the grass,* Katherine thought. Now the long-haired woman focused her dark eyes on the Band of Brocoudahl. Then she bowed her head.

"These are the people you told me about!" Katherine exclaimed.

The long-haired woman raised her head, smiling.

"We are the Terlooeth Teig, the People of the Plains. And when one courts our favor and friendship, we extend the Lady's Blessing." The woman's voice sounded like a melody played on a silver, open-holed flute.

"Moretta, Most Blessed," Wren said. "We ask for safe passage through the plains, and if possible, a place to rest from our travels."

Moretta's laughter tinkled like wind chimes in a soft summer breeze. "Wren's always welcome at the Sidhe. And his companions, too."

"Thank you, Moretta," Wren said. "If possible, I want to talk to Totatis."

Moretta nodded and made a slight hand motion. Her companions disappeared into the tall grass and Wren stepped aside to let the woman take the lead.

"Wren," Katherine whispered, grabbing Wren's arm. "Who are these people? When you told me about them, I expected them to be like us."

"They are like us."

"They're tiny and yellow!"

"They are still people, Katherine. I did not tell you what they looked like, because I did not think it important. Is it?"

"No, of course not." Katherine said, and Wren pulled her through the tall grass.

They came out of the grass atop a plateau. Katherine looked down toward the eastern banks of the Red River at a village of yellow buildings surrounded by a series of circular sun-washed gray stone walls. *Like a maze,* she thought.

All the Terlooeth Teig but the Most Blessed scurried down the steep bank toward the walls and vanished at the outermost wall. Before Katherine could ask where they disappeared to, the Most Blessed and Wren were halfway down the hill. Shaeff trotted by.

"Are you coming?"

Katherine noticed that she had stopped to stare, so she hurried after them.

At the wall, Moretta said, "To keep the People of the Plains safe, only those pure in thought can enter this most sacred Sidhe. If you erase from your mind all but the purpose that brought you here, it becomes easy to enter." She turned and gestured to Wren. "Now watch."

Wren stepped to the wall, moved into it, and disappeared. But the wall was solid! Then Moretta turned and gestured to Shaeff, who stepped up to the wall and disappeared instantly.

The Most Blessed now turned to Katherine.

Fearfully, Katherine reached out to touch the wall, but instead of stone felt a tingling not unlike the charge on an electric fence crawl over her skin. She looked down at the dark eyes that regarded her and then concentrated on Mandy, picturing her face with her dark eyes and impish smile. A charge drew her like a magnet, and she flowed forward, shutting her eyes tight, felt the woman's presence behind her, and thought, *Mandy!*

Blue lightning zigzagged behind her eyes and followed miles of nerve endings to touch every part of her being, and Katherine stumbled, dropped the Wand, and fell to her knees. When she raised her head and slowly opened her eyes, she was on flagstones with gray stone walls ten feet high on either side of a four-foot-wide corridor and open sky above. Wren was reaching his hand down to her. "Are you all right?" he asked.

Taking Wren's hand and standing up, she knew that she was inside the wall. But, she could not believe that those weird feelings had left her in one piece.

"What was that?"

The Most Blessed smiled gently and then bent down to pick up the Wand and hand it to her. "It is a spell that the Blue Sorcerers set to guard our village from unwanted visitors. The intricate walls surrounding the village draw Power to hold the spell in place indefinitely."

Then she led them between the walls, turning back again and again until Katherine's sense of direction became thoroughly confused. *This is a maze,* she thought and wondered how much longer they would have to walk until they came to the end of the design where, if her guess was right, the village would be.

Katherine finally stepped from the walled walkway onto a gravel path leading through a village of miniature stone houses with roofs thatched in yellow grass. Between the houses, children ran like golden fawns, their manes of white-gold hair dancing in the air. Wren talked to them in a language that sounded like the chirpings of meadowlarks and Shaeff playfully bounced after them.

The Most Blessed stopped in front of a house and motioned them inside. To avoid hitting the lintel, set at his chin level, Wren stooped to enter and Katherine followed into a room with walls covered in leather mats woven with painted clay beads, bones, and colored feathers. On the floor in the center of the room at a highly polished, low stone table, sat a wrinkled old man with long white hair. Before him was a pile of sticks like white ivory marked with black symbols.

When he glanced up, his dark eyes seemed full of wisdom and intelligence. Now, staring at Katherine, his eyes broadened. He stood up, bowed to Katherine, and spoke in whistles and peeps with Wren.

"You are not what Totatis pictured you to be," Wren said.

Totatis sat, scooped up then scattered the sticks across the table. Katherine was shocked when next he spoke.

"When I tossed the divination sticks, they revealed that the Seeker, wearing the Band of Brocoudahl, would come needing our aid," he said, pointing a gnarled finger at the sticks. "So I sent the Most Blessed to watch for your arrival."

The Most Blessed turned and left the hut.

Totatis gestured toward the floor around the table where scattered pillows lay.

"Now come and rest," he said. Katherine needed no second invitation.

Moretta returned with food and after they ate, Wren told Totatis about Katherine's search for Mandy. Then Totatis asked, "Would you like me to read the sticks for you, Katherine? Is there something that you would like to know about your daughter?"

Katherine felt a lump in the back of her throat. There were so many things she wanted to know. *Is Mandy all right? Is she eating right? Does she miss me? So many things!*

Totatis peered intently into Katherine's face.

"I cannot answer all your questions, Katherine. Just one."

What do I ask? she thought. *What do I need to know the most?* She racked her brain. The Wanderer's Wand was showing her which direction to go, but until Katherine found Mandy, how would she know her daughter was all right?

"I guess is she safe? Can I ask that?" She looked at Wren. He shrugged and looked at Totatis.

"The reading will only tell us what is true at this particular moment."

"So, what do I do?"

"Kneel here; you must face south and take the sticks and hold them in your hands. Concentrate on your question."

Katherine picked up the sticks. Their smooth sides felt cool to the touch. Totatis closed his eyes and chanted:

"Lord Dagda, Lady Brighid,

"As we cast the lots,

"Bless these hands—

"Rend the veil,

"Let us Far See

"Beyond our mortal lands."

He opened his eyes and looked at her.

"Now toss the sticks on the table, Katherine." The sticks clattered onto the tabletop.

"And repeat after me: Urd," he said.

"Urd."

"Verth."

"Verth."

"Skull," Totatis said.

"Skull." Katherine wondered what the words meant. She looked at the sticks. Some were lying face up with the strange black lines showing and others were face down, their white sides showing.

"Turn all the sticks face down, Katherine," Totatis said. "Shuffle them in a circle to your left. Good. Now pick three sticks and put them on the table in front of you and turn them face up."

Katherine did as she was told and then looked up at Totatis. His eyes were wide.

"What is it?" she asked.

"The sticks say her father hunts her."

"Her father hunts her?" She was not with her father! Then where was she? Was Mandy alone on this strange world? Katherine sobbed hysterically, put her head down on the table, couldn't stop crying. She felt as if she had been holding the tears back forever, and now that they were freed, she couldn't pull them back.

Soon she felt someone lift her, cradle her, and lower her onto a cushioned pallet. She opened her eyes to see Wren. *Mandy's in danger and I must find her,* she thought, *so why am I wasting time here?*

CHAPTER TWENTY-FIVE

BEHOLD! THE WIZARD WATER CHURNS AND TURNS THE SEEKER FROM HER PATH.

The next morning along the Red River, Katherine scrambled up a moss-covered rock to stand beside Wren. The sun on her left spread pink and orange light over the base of a plateau where a broad waterway thundered around a sweeping curve that crossed directly in front of them. The thought of having to cross the river brought back memories of crossing the waterfall. *If I managed that,* she shrugged, *I can manage this.*

Wren pointed. "There's the ferry."

A boat bobbing in the water was secured to shore with a hemp rope tied to a stout timber. The rope threaded through a pulley attached to each end of the flat-bottomed boat and then stretched across the river to another timber on the far bank, a hundred yards away. Katherine eyed the boat warily. Wren tossed in their gear and settled Katherine into a seat. Shaeff nestled between her feet and packs. Wren loosed the mooring and stepped behind the bow seat.

"Is this safe?" Katherine asked.

"Just relax. It will be all right!" Wren answered. Then his back to her, he braced his legs against the bow seat and pulled the rope.

The craft bounced away from the platform and rocked in the current. Water slapped hard against the boat's sides and Katherine was splashed by it. She smelled fish and vegetation. Looking down, she saw water pooling on the boat's flat bottom and pulled her feet up cross-legged to avoid soaking her boots. Water hit the boat's sides and splashed her again.

"Wren, everything's getting wet."

"The food is in watertight wraps," Wren said. "Anything else that gets wet will dry. Including you."

He lunged forward and pulled the rope. The boat rocked forward and this time, the water crashed against the boat's sides with a jolt that snapped Katherine to attention. Sitting up, she panned the distance to the far bank. It seemed to be taking Wren forever to move the boat a few feet forward and already the back of his shirt was soaked with sweat, and his breath was growing ragged. Katherine suddenly realized that the rope was the only thing holding them in place. Her pulse quickened and beads of sweat formed under the Band on her forehead.

"Do you want help, Wren?"

"Not yet," he grunted. He leaned into the rope and braced his legs against the forward seat and pulled. The boat barely moved.

"It is never this hard," Wren said pulling hard on the rope. "Something's wrong." The boat bounced up and down in the middle of the river, like a fishing bob.

"We're going to make it, aren't we?" Katherine asked.

"Certainly." But Wren didn't sound certain.

Water flailed the bottom of the boat, and Shaeff whined. The current was trying to tear the rocking boat from the rope. Leaning into the rope, Wren bent across the seat to examine the front pulley. Then the rope snapped and Wren fell. Katherine heard Wren's head rap against the pulley pole. The current grabbed the boat, spinning it down river as she watched him fall precariously against the boat's edge. She tried to stand to gain the leverage needed to pull Wren back, but the prow plummeted. She slipped to her knees on the planking, then slid backward on the bottom of the boat with Wren's dead weight on top of her.

Cold water crashed over the sides of the boat, soaking her. They bumped into a boulder, spun and hit another, then turned and tumbled on down river, going faster. She eased out from under Wren's seemingly lifeless body. Cold water dashed against the bow, and the shoreline seemed a watery blur. The boat was speeding down river now, and Wren lie unconscious on his back, face a pasty white, lips blue. The water frothed and splashed over the side, rattling the Wand against the boards in the few inches of water on the boat's bottom. The boat rocked and hit a boulder with a crunch, spun around, tipped down, and then plunged through a narrow divide into a churning cauldron of white water that splashed into her eyes and mouth.

Then she heard a low, massive rumbling.

"What is it?" she asked.

"Wizard water."

She wondered at Shaeff's words and then knew.

"Rapids! Wren! Wake up!" she screamed.

Water boiled over the boat and crashed over her. She spit out brackish water. Then the bow dived into the water and slammed up, and she was flung backward against the seat. Sparks flew behind her eyes, and her fingers felt numb. The boat tipped and rolled as if plummeting down a waterslide and darkness hurled toward her like a giant wave. She heard Shaeff from far away.

"Katherine! Hold on!"

CHAPTER TWENTY-SIX

THE POWERS OF SPIRIT
HELP THE SEEKER THROUGH THE NIGHT.

Katherine opened her eyes to a purple-gray canopy of lush vegetation obstructing her view of the sky. Below the leaves were huge trunks, their thick branches draped with long streamers of lace-like brown moss and vines. Rising from indigo water at the base of tree trunks were gnarled clusters of green grass, clumps of emerald ferns, and curls of soft, gray mist. Katherine wrinkled her nose at the smell of rotting vegetation in the hot motionless air. She sat up and waited for the pain at the back of her head to subside. She was sitting in the boat, its bow torn away, its aft beached on a shelf of gray sand.

Midges darted around her head, bottle flies landed on her arms, and dragonflies, like flying rainbows, skimmed across water that sparkled in splotches of sunlight. She raised her arm to ward off the insects swarming around her and noticed Wren's pack on the water-logged boat's planking. Where was he? And Shaeff? Wren would never have left her alone if he had been all right.

She turned her head to look for them, and the quick movement sent another sharp pain through her head. *Do I wait here and hope they come for me, or do I try to go on without them?* She could not find her way on her own and poisonous snakes might lurk beneath the water plants. She felt like crying.

She dug into the pack and swallowed some of Wren's Nightroot. It would not hurt to take an extra swallow, she thought, and tipped the canteen up again.

"Katherine!" Wren's voice startled her, and she turned to see him tramping toward her across gray sand.

"Are you all right?" she called.

Wren nodded and held up a handful of green leafy plants, the roots dangling black dirt. "Featherfoil." He tossed the plants beside the boat and sat on the sand in front of her.

"I was afraid you had left me," she said.

"But, I never left you alone, Katherine. See?"

He pointed beside her. Shaeff, his nose resting against forepaws, was stretched out a few feet from the stern of the beached boat, sleeping in the sand.

"How do you feel?" Wren asked. "You were unconscious a long time."

"My head hurts, but I'm all right. Where are we?"

"Monad Marsh, which drains south into Pearl Lake." He picked up a featherfoil plant, tore a leaf into three long strips, and wove them together. The braided plant he tied around Katherine's wrist.

"What is this for?" she asked. He then tied one around his own wrist.

"It is a ward, Katherine, to keep us from sickness."

"What's a ward?"

"A ward is a type of magic that prevents something from happening. The marsh is filled with insects and plants that can cause sickness, and featherfoil keeps sickness away magically."

A week ago, Katherine never would have believed him, but with everything that she'd been through since, she was glad to wear the featherfoil bracelet. He handed Katherine the Wand.

"Give us a direction in which to start walking."

Katherine positioned the Wand in front of her. She whispered Mandy's name and adjusted her position until the crystal glowed with a steady white flame.

"Is that west?"

"Yes," Wren said, but he was not pleased. "Directly west lies Rockfang Rift, a desert in the middle of Wry. Nothing grows there, and there is no water or shade. I doubt that Mandy is there. But, if she is with Kylasar at the Keep far west of the Rift, then we must either go across or around it. Since I know no one survives the Rift, then I suggest we go south first, then west."

Katherine had no idea what Wren was talking about. She only knew that the Wand pointed west. If that was where Mandy was, then they should go in that direction.

"We must go west, Wren. Mandy is there."

"Katherine, look." Wren said, "We are here at Monad Marsh." He took a featherfoil branch and drew an X in the sand in front of her. "This is west and the Shadowspawn Mountains," and he drew another X to the left of the first one. "In between lies Rockfang Rift." He drew a wavy line dividing the two. "We cannot go west from here. We have to first go south. The only road that heads west is at the southern tip of Rockfang Rift."

Then from the Wand's crystal a white spark crackled, and arced to the sand on top of the X marking Monad Marsh. It moved southward in a curve under the line Wren dubbed as Rockfang Rift, then angled up across the ground to stop northwest of the second X. With a puff of smoke it was gone, leaving only a black smudge on the sand.

"Look, Katherine," Wren said. "The smudged line starts at Monad Marsh, follows a southern route around the Rift to move west toward Shadowspawn Mountains, then ends just north where Tradertown would be."

"Then that must be where Mandy is!"

"But I have not traveled that far before," Wren said, looking apprehensive. "It is Kylasar's domain."

"But if Mandy is there, then that is where we go!"

Katherine stretched over the boat's rail and rubbed Shaeff behind his ear.

"First we have to get through Monad Marsh," Wren spoke softly. "Snap Jaws in the water can swallow you whole. Choker Worms can drop from branches and latch onto your skin. And, Spidernet Trees can pull you into their huge mouths. All of these things move very quickly, like lightning."

"I wish Serhonydd had come with us," she said.

Wren looked up from poking the sand with the branch.

"Perhaps, but Serhonydd is not here, so you will have to make do with us." He smiled. "Is that so bad?"

Katherine wondered if she had hurt Wren's feelings.

"Wren, don't misunderstand me. Serhonydd's arrogant and a little moody—two traits that fortunately you haven't got. But he seemed very knowledgeable about Wry, and he seemed to want to help us. The more help we can get, the better I feel."

"I must admit I feel safer myself with Serhonydd around. He has an aura of power."

"That he does not use," Shaeff interjected.

"He made his own choice, Shaeff," Wren said. "He was the youngest mage ever on Wry. I have heard stories of great feats of magic that he performed for the nobility of Wry's Ken before he was ten."

"Such as?" Katherine prompted.

"Creating illusions of great flying dragons and conjuring rose-colored crystal goblets inlaid with silver and filled with nightroot that a person could actually drink! But, his most famous feat was shape shifting into a golden phoenix."

To Katherine, Serhonydd seemed a little like Mozart, a creative prodigy. What would have happened had Mozart given up his music?

After they set up camp and settled in for the night, it was a long time before the crickets and tree frogs quieted. As she tried to go to sleep, Katherine wondered whether she would ever see Mandy again.

CHAPTER TWENTY-SEVEN

O DRU'DAMMEN—PRIDE CAN MASK THE TRUTH WITHIN THE SOUL.

In the waning light, Serhonydd studied the rope trailing from the timber brace into the surge of dark river. He looked among the tangle of mottled vegetation at the far bank but failed to find the missing ferry. If the boat had snapped free from the rope, it would have traveled downstream through the wizard water, and if Katherine and Wren were alive, they would end up in Monad Marsh. Serhonydd swore at himself. He never should have allowed Katherine to start her journey without him. He turned south to look for the ferry boat along the riverbanks, fervently wishing he could regain the peace he had before Katherine entered his life.

When he had abruptly left the room like a spoiled child with Katherine watching, he had felt angry that his decision to avoid the power had been undermined by his parents. They said time and time again that they only wanted what was best for him. Yet who knew better what was best for him than himself? After ten years of peace with his decision, why was he now wondering whether that decision had been wrong? He had resented the times they had left him to roam the countryside to fight Kylasar's legions. When he was five, Serhonydd had wanted to go everywhere with his parents. They had said that too many dangers lurked outside Wry's Ken for a boy his age. Maybe they had been overly protective, but he had hated being left behind with tutors. Then when they told him it was time to take the Power, he had refused. Could he have rationalized himself into not wanting the Power simply because it was what they wanted? If they had not been Blue Sorcerers and had asked him not to take up the Power, would he have thwarted their wishes and become a Sorcerer to spite them?

The ground beneath his feet grew soggy, and farther south he could see wet marshland sprouting with clusters of tall rushes. He failed to see any evidence that Katherine and Wren had passed this way. Maybe they had swum to shore long before.

When a shriek from a diving crane startled him, Serhonydd looked up to see storm clouds billowing over the plateau on his left. He had come miles with his thoughts elsewhere and silently berated himself for not paying closer attention to the sides of the riverbank along the way. Under the darkening sky, the once pounding river on his right now flattened out before him into lazy rills, reflecting the last rays of light and spreading like splayed white fingers under dark green vegetation.

Night and its darkness descended upon him, and insects, swamp frogs, crickets, and birds with their nocturnal thrumming, chirping, trilling, and whistling encircled him. Against calm sounds of water lapping over soft earth, now and then an owl's hoot echoed that of its far-off neighbor.

Maybe I should look for Katherine using the True Path spirit sighting, Serhonydd thought. If he could find her aura, then he would at least know whether she were still alive. He stopped, sat on a small flat stone at the placid water's edge, and moved into the True Path position with his legs crossed, his elbows on his knees. He knew spirit sighting would leave his body unprotected, but few predators in this region would bother a human. *Only a Rathrider,* he thought morbidly. And he had read in Balsak's book that Kylasar could not send his Power to a far-off location without obsidian rock there to focus through. Here along the river, the rock was shale. Closing his eyes, trying to relax, Serhonydd cleansed his mind of all thoughts of the world around him. He breathed with his diaphragm, expanding his chest as he inhaled, shoving his stomach toward his spine as he exhaled. Sounds began to fade. He searched his mind for his spirit, which he imagined as a tiny mote of light within his conscious. Serhonydd concentrated on finding this light.

Suddenly, he felt as if he were floating, turning, end over end, down a deep, dark well. Watching this imagined well slide by, he noticed how each stone in the wall joined its neighbor like a puzzle piece. He drew his eye along mortar cracks and lines toward the blue-black pool of ever-widening circles at the well's bottom. The smallest circle, surrounded with light, widened until Serhonydd saw his reflection on the surface. Like a snake shedding its skin floating in water, his spirit, attached to his body by a silver gossamer thread, slipped free. This thread would pull him back to his body when he needed to return. But if stretched too far, the thread would break, Serhonydd's body would die, and his spirit would be lost forever.

Now, still in the True Path position, Serhonydd hovered above his body. Seeing that no danger lurked near his physical self, Serhonydd turned toward the swamp in search of Katherine. He skimmed over marshland, glowing like verdigris on copper. Snakes slid across rushes into the gelid water, black spiders tripped across thin webs to pounce on dragonflies, and sharp-beaked birds darted to snatch fish from the water. Like a soft wind blowing through marsh grass, his spirit self passed deep within the grass through the very cells where life pulsated with blue, green, and violet sparks, but he was looking for a brighter spark, one that would draw him like a beacon. The silver thread was stretching thin.

The sparks swirled into darker blue, green, and violet bands and Serhonydd knew he could not search much longer without damaging his body. All motion around him ceased, and the colors settled into the blue of still water, the green of marsh grass, and the violet of tiny blossoms growing beneath the grass. He must turn back. But then a red spark blinked near the corner of his eye and a corona of red glowed brighter than the other sparks around a sleeping form. Katherine! Wren, his aura a deep golden yellow, was asleep next to her with Shaeff curled in slumber at his feet.

Drawing near, Serhonydd hovered, watching her struggle to get comfortable while she slept on the broken boat. Her crimson aura flashed like rays of a red, morning sun and told him that she was filled with a vigorous intensity, alive and safe. Reluctant to leave Katherine, Serhonydd nevertheless thought to follow the silver thread and instantly returned back to his body.

Some foul evil lurked close to Katherine; he had sensed it in the mist. Opening his eyes, Serhonydd stretched, picked up his pack and walking stick, and as fast as possible, with his leather boots splashing ankle-deep in water, he headed south into the marsh.

CHAPTER TWENTY-EIGHT

WITH POWER THE SEEKER'S IRE ENFLAMES AND BURNS THE DEMON.

Katherine woke with a start.

"The day is here," Wren said, and motioned toward the marsh.

Katherine's clothes stuck to her body, but her bare toes felt good when she wiggled them. Last night she had taken off her wet boots and placed her socks over the boat rail to dry. Now, she pulled dry socks over dirty feet, plunged her feet into her boots, and followed Wren into the marsh.

"How long will it take to get out of here?" she asked.

Wren and Shaeff exchanged a look.

"By evening, if we are lucky." He handed Katherine the Wand. "Don't forget to watch out for Snap Jaws. They look like mottled tree trunks moving through the water."

Like alligators? Katherine shivered. She did not want to run into one, whatever they looked like. The cold water quickly seeped through her boots and leggings, and weighed her down. She sank in soft mud and struggled through water and over roots, lifting her legs high to break the suction underfoot. She constantly had to brush aside hanging moss.

"Beware of Choker Worms, Katherine," Shaeff said. *"They hang over branches and look like thick indigo vines."*

Snakes? She thought, *I hate snakes.*

Perspiration, running down her back and along her jaw, attracted midges, and frustrated, she splashed the fetid marsh water on her face. It helped. The midges stayed around her head, not on her face.

She grew exhausted watching for Snap Jaws and Choker Worms, and her head began to ache. Wren surprised a flock of azure-colored birds the size of hawks. Screeching, they ascended into the air and then swooped toward her. Katherine raised her arms to protect her face and eyes and splashed toward Wren. Unable to stop her forward momentum, she stumbled into him, and they both went into the water. When they managed to extricate themselves from each other and from the mud, an angry shriek startled them. They sat still watching the bird settle on the ground beside them to pick mites from under its wing.

"Let us see if we can find a dry spot," Wren said.

Shaeff splashed over to Wren.

"There is a large shelf fungus ahead."

Within minutes they arrived at a large tree, with roots rising six feet from the marsh. Above the roots, around a trunk like a cardboard collar grew a bright yellow fungus nearly a foot thick and three feet wide.

Wren formed a stirrup with his hands and hoisted Katherine over the edge of the smooth, almost rubbery surface of fungus. It felt good to be out of the marsh water. Shaeff jumped up, Katherine helping him, and he started to shake the water out of his fur. It tickled her nose, and she sneezed.

Shaeff licked her face. *"Thanks."*

"Just don't gain any more weight."

Wren scrambled onto the fungus.

The sun had risen higher in the sky, and the vegetation around her was a dozen shades of green. Katherine watched bright blue birds swoop under thick underbrush and fly out and back again. Overhead, delicate moss formed a curtain-like mosquito netting of fine, interlocking lace. Katherine removed her boots and spread her socks on the fungus to dry. Her feet were blistered and swollen.

After they ate, Katherine watched yellow and red butterflies chase each other across the mud. Dragonflies chased the butterflies and then flittered low across turquoise water.

"How can something as deadly as you say the marsh is be so beautiful?" Katherine asked aloud.

"Look!" Wren said, "A Snap Jaw!"

An animal looking very much like an alligator, its skin glittering like a faceted emerald, broke the water. Its broad snout with sharp, jagged teeth snapped around a blue bird.

"Then again," she turned and smiled at Wren, "how can something as beautiful as the marsh be so deadly?"

"It all depends on your point of view," Wren said. "Take you and Kylasar, for instance. Here on Wry, we have always known Kylasar to be evil, a mad sorcerer searching for a way to rule the whole world. Yet you come to our world and tell us that you have never known the man to be evil."

"He is just a man, Wren," Katherine said quietly. "No more evil than anyone else."

"Now, that is my point. From your point of view, Kylasar appears to be a normal man."

"So why don't you tell me your view of Kylasar?" she asked.

Wren focused his blue eyes on her.

"I do not think you really want to hear it, Katherine."

"Please, it's important to me."

Wren looked toward the marsh.

"I am not learned like Serhonydd. I cannot read or write, so what I tell you may or may not be written in the Book of Belanos in the Archives, yet it is what people say and have said about Kylasar ever since I can remember."

"The Dark One known as Loche
"God of Chaos, Mankind's Bane
"Summons power while his Flesh
"Lies trapped on Twisted Plane—
"While this evil lives in Kylasar
"His Darkness drowns the Light
"And Wry crumbles. Death comes
"To Lord Dagda and Lady Brighid."

"What does that mean?" Katherine asked.

"That Kylasar and Loche, the God of Chaos, are working together to destroy the world."

"On my world, Loche's name is Lucifer," Katherine said.

"That's impossible, Katherine," Wren objected. "He may be a god, but he cannot be in two places at once, can he?"

"I don't know. Why?"

"Because according to legends, Lord Dagda banished Loche to the Twisted Plane and hid him away from all the world. At that time, all evil went with him. But somehow, over the centuries, his evil has leaked back into the world. We Yttoshamen believe Kylasar to be the focus of Loche's evil. Once Kylasar spent all his magical efforts on reinforcing his Black Guard, building weapons of war, controlling the coffers of the Church, and subjugating my people. We Yttoshamen believe that lately Kylasar's priorities have changed."

"Why would you think that?"

"Because Kylasar doesn't train his Black Guard like he used to; he hasn't waged a major campaign in the past few years, he hasn't enforced our paying coin to the Church lately, and he doesn't seem interested in what we do. He only hunts for the One-Horne. Remember Lady A'legra said that the One-Horne carried a locket that Lord Dagda and Lady Brighid put something into. Well, I believe that the Jeweled Locket contains a potion, a spell, something that will release Loche from the Twisted Plane. If that is true, and Kylasar locates the One-Horne, then he could free Loche. Together, Loche and Kylasar would rule Wry."

"Why don't Lord Dagda and Lady Brighid step in and get rid of Kylasar?"

"They brought you here to thwart him, did they not?"

Startled, Katherine looked up sharply at Wren. She hardly believed that Wren's gods would want her as their champion to stop an evil sorcerer from unleashing the God of Chaos on this world.

"What you think is ludicrous, Wren. I suppose that could explain how I came to Wry, but … I'm not magical, and I can't fight a sorcerer! And, if Kylasar is Eric, as you all seem to think, then I won't fight him. He always got his way by either threatening or bashing me. If I never fought him when I was married to him, what would make me fight him now?"

"Your wanting Mandy back."

Katherine shuddered. If taking Mandy home meant a physical confrontation with Eric, then she supposed she would fight, fight until she was too beaten to move. He must not win. Not as long as she still had breath inside to fight.

"You are the Seeker, Katherine. Wry's fate depends on you," Wren said. "I think we should be going."

Back in the water, Katherine could not believe that the fate of Wry depended on her. What could she do against a sorcerer in control of demons and Rathriders? She was not really sure that she was even capable of finding Mandy and taking her home. If Wren thought that she was the Seeker, well, let him think that.

Katherine had no illusions as to who she was. She was merely a mother in search of her missing child. The fact that she had somehow stumbled into another world changed nothing. A person was the same no matter what environment she was placed in.

She had not been able to oppose Eric the first time she met him. With pizzas and Cokes, Eric and a friend had come banging on the door at her girlfriend's, and studying for a biology final had turned into an all-night gab session. Eric's long auburn hair and dark eyes had made her think of Heathcliff in *Wuthering Heights*. Had she been under a spell at the time? It had not felt like a spell. She had merely fallen in love with him. But, wasn't falling in love a spell? Katherine shook her head. Trying to think about Eric was like trudging through the brackish water and mud that sucked at her feet and slowed her down. Moss hung like ragged curtains from overhanging branches laden with leaves like elephant-ears. Tired of swatting the bottle flies on her eyes and mouth, she covered her face with her hands.

Then Wren disappeared as if he had fallen down a well. In her terror, she lost her footing and slipped completely under the fetid water. Spewing and coughing, she struggled back to her feet in time to see a long reddish brown snake torpedo toward her. Screaming, she thrashed blindly toward the bank where she had last seen Wren.

"Stop!"

Shaeff's mental command was too late to keep her from a shimmering tangle of neon green vine that snapped like steel coils around her neck. She dropped the Wand and clawed helplessly with both hands to pull the vine from her neck. She gasped for air. Black dots swam before her eyes and her lungs burned for oxygen. The pressure was released and she choked, gasping, relieved to breathe again and her vision cleared. Then she was yanked ten feet into the air to hang upside down. She screamed, again.

Her vision dimming, she saw Wren running toward her as if in slow motion. Terrified, Katherine twisted around. The vines that held her were like green laser light filaments spewing from the treetop. The vines jerked her closer to a gaping hole in the tree. The smell was sickening, like rotten meat. Shaeff barked and whined, jumping and snapping at the vines. Katherine could see Wren hacking the vines with his knife, but she was moving closer to the gaping maw. She needed a knife to cut through the vines holding her.

"Wren!" she screamed, "Throw me the knife!"

Wren threw the knife, but she fumbled, and it fell back to earth. The vines tightened and wrenched her closer to the ever widening gap in the trunk. The leather bag once under her shirt now banged against her chin, her Dad's lighter and key clicking together. *Dad's lighter!* she thought. She pulled the lighter from the bag, flicked it into a flame, and held the flame to a vine. To her joy, the vine recoiled, but in recoiling knocked from her hand the lighter that fell to the ground below.

"Wren!" she yelled, "throw me the lighter!"

Only a foot away from her face, the bile-green interior of the gaping maw churned a putrid substance. Katherine fought to keep from vomiting. Wren stood transfixed, the lighter at his feet. Then she remembered his fear of fire.

"Please, Wren—" she begged between clenched teeth, "the lighter won't hurt you."

The vines burned like acid on her skin, and her face moved mere inches from the maw. Shaeff tugged on Wren's leggings.

A figure in a dark cloak swept through the ferns, scooped up the lighter, and instantly, flames encompassed the vines holding her. A high-pitched squeal burst from deep inside the trunk, and the vines dropped Katherine head first onto the soft muddy ground. The writhing and snaking vines curled and withered into blackened stubs and, with a sound like a wooden box lid closing, the maw snapped shut.

Serhonydd's dark robes swirled toward Katherine, and when she began to cry, he pulled her close.

CHAPTER TWENTY-NINE

O CHILDE, YOUR MOTHER WONDERS WHERE—YOU LAY YOUR SLEEPY HEAD.

Mandy sat with her back against a scrawny pine tree, her hands tied together in her lap. When she smelled Gunta's stew cooking over the camp fire in the middle of the clearing, she shuddered. The days traveling with Gunta and Punquod were a patchwork of donkey smells, bad food, and sleepless nights. She did not know how long they had been traveling, but she felt as if she had been smelly, hungry, and sleepy, forever.

Punquod stretched on the ground behind the fire, his eyes closed. Gunta ladled dark-brown stew onto dirt-encrusted dishes, and thrust the rank-smelling stew under her nose. She knew that she had to eat the rank stew or die from hunger. There hadn't been any bread for days.

"I can't eat with my hands tied, Gunta," Mandy said.

Gunta set the dish on the ground and retied her left hand to her right ankle. After taking her first taste, she almost gagged. She blinked fast, trying to not let Gwenydd see her tears. But Gwenydd was hungrily scraping her dish clean with her fingers.

From a stand of pines behind her, the donkeys twitched their ears and brayed. Then Mandy heard an unfamiliar snort. Twigs loudly snapped and pebbles clattered. Alarmed, Gunta jerked his stubby sword up, accidently slicing through his rope belt. His pants fell around his knees, and without the belt holding it, Gunta's scrap-metal chest protector slid off, bounced, and spun across the ground like a top. Punquod, now on his feet, brandished his sword in a long sweeping arc in the direction where Gunta peered. They both looked scared. Bending over to pull up his pants, Gunta backed into Punquod's sword tip. "Ahhh!" he bellowed, fell face forward and dropped his short sword.

A man dressed in silver-green rode a white-maned chestnut mare into the clearing. He stopped before Gunta's prone figure and held the reins in one hand and an axe in the other. To Gwenydd and Mandy, he gave a friendly nod. *Things are definitely looking up,* Mandy thought. Had her father sent him to rescue her? He had amber eyes in a tan face and long golden-brown hair braided with a leather thong and brown and white bird feathers. Gunta seemed frozen tight to the ground and Punquod, the whites of his eyes enormous, had lowered his sword to his side.

"Who's in charge here?" the man asked.

Punquod took a step backward.

The man raised the axe.

"Stand your ground."

Punquod quailed.

"You there," the man called to Gunta. "Are you in charge?"

Gunta inched his hand toward his fallen sword, and quicker than Mandy thought possible, the man in silver-green slid from his saddle and landed a boot on Gunta's reaching fingers.

"My fingers!" Gunta whined. The man retrieved Gunta's sword from the ground. He waved the sword at Gunta.

"Get up."

Gunta stood, forgetting that his pants were around his ankles. Mandy tried not to laugh.

"Your sword, please?" the man asked Punquod, and he meekly relinquished his blade.

CHAPTER THIRTY

THE PATH WILL TWIST THE WAY FOR HE WHO YEARNS FOR TRUTH.

Behind his companions, Serhonydd trudged west along Minstrel's Way, the road toward the Shadowspawn Mountains. It had been three days since the Spidernet tree attacked Katherine, and from the moment he had held her, Serhonydd had known that he was very much in love with this woman from another world. Now Serhonydd worried about her, for the tree's vines contained a poison that had infected her blood. Serhonydd was thankful that Wren had had the foresight to braid her a featherfoil bracelet. Its magic power had diluted the poison and would probably save her life.

Last night he had noticed that Katherine's speech had grown slurred, and this morning she appeared weak. Now she stumbled in front of him. Wren caught and eased her to the ground. Perspiration glistened on her fever-flushed forehead, and her breathing was slow and labored. Serhonydd felt Wren's resentment in thinking that he could heal Katherine if he would use the Power. Would I use the Power? Yes, he would gladly use whatever Power he had to save her life. He prayed that it would not come down to that.

"We must stop, Serhonydd," Wren said. He lifted Katherine into his arms and looked to the roadside. "She cannot be moved until the poison has run its course."

CHAPTER THIRTY-ONE

BEDAZZLED SIGHT, O FAERIE DREAM, THE ONE-HORNE COMES TO CALL.

Astride the donkey, Mandy rode in cool late-morning shadows under massive branches following Jorn, who had led them now for four days. Brightly colored birds twittered and flittered from branch to branch. Mandy wondered if Punquod and Gunta had escaped after Jorn tied them up. She knew that she should feel sorry for them, but she didn't. It had been much nicer traveling with Jorn. He was always smiling and joking. He never shouted or threatened. He didn't smell, and he had lots of good food to eat. Best of all, he was taking them to Keepsburg. Now if she could find a phone and talk to her mother, then everything would be all right. Mandy glanced back at Gwenydd, who struggled to keep her donkey under control. Gwenydd's hair was full of tangles, and the freckles on her face stood out against sunburned skin. When they came to a sunlit clearing, they dismounted for a lunch of journey cake and Jorn told Gwenydd for the tenth time how the One-Horne sent him to find them. But today when Jorn mentioned Mandy's father, Gwenydd looked frightened and had stopped with the journey cake halfway to her mouth.

"What?" Mandy asked.

"I said Kylasar gave me an arrow," Jorn swallowed.

"Kylasar is my father," Mandy said.

"Your *father*?" Jorn blanched. No wonder Mandy reminded him of someone. She had the same dark eyes as Kylasar. *If I take her to Kylasar,* Jorn thought, *he will kill me for not finding the One-Horne.*

Mandy saw the same look on Jorn's face that had crossed Gwenydd's at the Keep when she had mentioned her father. *What do they know that I don't?* she wondered. She was afraid to ask, but more afraid of not asking.

"What is wrong with my father?" she whispered.

Gwenydd looked at Jorn, then back to Mandy.

"Remember when you said your father would never beat you?"

"Yes," Mandy answered.

"Well, I didn't say anything then. But once when I spilt a tray in the hall, your father slapped me, hard, and he said that if my clumsiness ever displeased him again, he would feed me to the dogs."

Mandy jumped to her feet. *How could Gwenydd be so mean?* she thought. *My father would never act that way. Never!*

"Take it back, Gwenydd!"

Gwenydd began to sob, and Mandy grew confused. Gwenydd had helped her escape from the Keep, and if her father had threatened her, then Gwenydd was a true friend who had risked everything to help. Mandy thought that perhaps her father was the reason Gwenydd had wanted to escape from the Keep.

Gwenydd wiped her eyes on her shirt sleeve. "It's true! Ask Jorn."

"Your father is the Dark Imperator, Lady Amanda," Jorn said. He wondered how much he should tell the girl. "Everyone is afraid of him, myself included."

"How can you be afraid of him, Jorn?" Mandy asked.

"I have seen him hurt people." Jorn dusted his palms together and began to pack the food away.

"My father? Hurt people?" She had never seen her father physically hurt anyone. But then she started to remember something that had happened to her mother a long time ago, when her father had yelled at her. What was it?

"How?" she demanded, blinking the tears back.

"With his magic."

"Magic?"

"He is a sorcerer, Lady Amanda," Jorn said quietly.

"Sorcerers are in fairy tales," Mandy said, her anger rising again.

"Sorcerers happen in Wry, too, Lady Amanda," Gwenydd said.

Mandy was terribly confused. She had thought this place was just the other side of Pittsburgh, but the Keep was built like a castle and the craerlytes created light. Keepsburg had no cars or telephones. Punquod and Gunta wanted to sell her and Gwenydd as slaves. And the One-Horne, if she could believe Jorn, had spoken to him. Those things were not on the other side of Pittsburgh.

And, her father. Mandy had never doubted him before. Now she wondered. She recalled a time, during an argument, when her father had twisted her mother's arm. Later, she had worn a long-sleeved sweater to cover the bruises. Something snapped inside Mandy, and she remembered other times when her mother had been hurt by her father. *But he never hurt me,* she thought. *I wonder why not? He had been very strict, but never mean. Well, maybe sometimes. But he had never locked me in my room before.* The man who did that had been a stranger.

"This place is really strange. Why did my father bring me here? Something odd is going on. My father acts weird, but I don't believe he's a sorcerer. Gwenydd, it's impossible."

Jorn listened to the girls as he packed the food away. *What was he to do with Kylasar's daughter?* She trusted him and thought that they were heading back to Keepsburg. He had planned to take them there, but now he knew it was too dangerous for him. If they went to Keepsburg, they might be discovered and taken to Kylasar. If he could help Mandy find her mother, then he might not have to take her to Keepsburg. That way, he would not chance running into Kylasar.

"Mandy," he asked, "Where's your mother?"

"I don't know."

Mandy was getting scared. She had already asked Jorn if he knew where she could find a telephone and like Gwenydd, he didn't know what a telephone was. If Jorn didn't know, then she might never get home. She started to cry. She heard the pounding of hooves and turned to see a huge white horse race up the trail. From the center of the horse's forehead rose a golden horn at least a foot long, a horn that shone as bright as sunlight on water. At the edge of the clearing, the horse whinnied and lowered its long, white-maned head to the ground. When the horse lifted its head, a brightly colored jewel sparkled from a chain around its neck.

"It's the One-Horne, Mandy!" Gwenydd whispered.

Afraid that the light spilling from the golden horn would hypnotize her, Mandy blinked. The horse turned its head sideways. The horse had blue eyes! Did horses have blue eyes? She stepped forward to touch the One-Horne, wanting to ride like the wind on its back. The One-Horne nickered and then rose up on its hind legs. She stepped closer, and the One-Horne stood still, head lowered, blue eye watching as her hands moved to its neck. Her fingers touched the soft, silken skin and spread out, curled rubbing gently. The One-Horne nuzzled her cheek, and its warm breath tickled Mandy's neck. A gentle voice sounded in her mind.

"Take the necklace, Mandy."

She moved her hands down both sides of the horse's neck to the golden chain and lifted it over the One-Horne's head. The jewel was a tiny locket, about one-half inch thick and two or three inches in diameter. The front and back sides of the locket looked like little round stained-glass windows with gold between colored stones. When Mandy moved the locket, the stones sparkled and shone. The One-Horne nodded.

"Put it on."

And Mandy did.

CHAPTER THIRTY-TWO

TRUST IN WAND, KEY, BAND, AND LIGHTER, EARTH, AIR, WATER, FIRE.

In her fever, Katherine saw visions of vines with fingers like green tarantula legs and trees with witch-like faces gnashing razor teeth. Wren was miles beneath her, as if she were looking at him from the wrong end of a telescope, and Serhonydd was surrounded by a cloak of yellow flame that smothered her. Waking, she struggled to breathe and her lungs burned from heated air. *So thirsty,* she thought, and fell back to a dreamless sleep.

Much later, she felt her head being lifted, and when a cool liquid wet her lips, she opened her eyes. Then with a gentleness that Katherine had never noticed before, she heard Serhonydd say, "Not too much," and she saw the shape of his face hovering over her in the dark.

"What happened?" she whispered.

Serhonydd eased her head down. "You've been ill." He washed her face with a cool wet cloth.

She cleared her throat. "How long?"

"It's the night of the second day since you were poisoned by the vines of the Spidernet Tree. But your fever has broken."

When Katherine next opened her eyes, her skin felt cool, and she could swallow without her throat burning. The morning sky was filled with soft pinks and purples. Birds chirped and rustled through green-leaved tree branches some fifteen feet above her head. She could smell bacon frying and, suddenly, hunger gnawed at her. Slowly she sat up. Wren speared a slice of bacon sizzling on a faerlyte griddle. Behind him, on a log with Shaeff at his feet, sat Serhonydd.

After she ate, Katherine felt Serhonydd's blue eyes regarding her. "Totatis did a divination for me, and the sticks said that Mandy's father was looking for her. She must be on her own somewhere on Wry!"

"I know," he said. "Wren told me."

Katherine picked up the Wand, and when she called for Mandy, the crystal's light glowed. Looking at Serhonydd, she had a sudden insight. "You know where Mandy is, don't you?" she asked.

"Totatis was right," Serhonydd said. "If Mandy were with Kylasar at the Keep, then the Wand would be pointing northwest, but the Wand points directly west." He rubbed his hands together and smiled at Katherine. "It is a good omen for us. If Mandy has already escaped Kylasar's grasp, our chances of finding her have improved a hundredfold."

Katherine brushed her bangs back, felt the Band of Brocoudahl around her forehead, and remembered the vision that she had seen when she first found the Band. Again she heard the simple series of musical notes that had led her to the white light that room in her mind filled with power, power she might need if Mandy were not with Kylasar.

"Then let's hurry, Serhonydd; we have to find her before Kylasar does!"

Serhonydd watched Katherine gather her gear to continue her quest. Her eyes no longer had that vacant dullness in them that he had seen the past few days. She had recovered, and he felt good. He picked up his pack and walking stick.

CHAPTER THIRTY-THREE

BEYOND THE GARGOYLES OF GNEISS THE LAND BELONGS TO KYLASAR.

Serhonydd vaguely remembered passing this way, Minstrel Way, the road that led east to west over hills through the southern tip of Whisperwood Forest years ago. Near the edges of the white sandy road and under the tree trunks were thin blades of pine green grass and splashes of yellow, blue, and red wildflowers. The mottled brown trunks and dark emerald leaves of huge, straight trees were spotted yellow with sunlight. The rising sun behind him heated his back through his robe.

"Oh, look at that!" Katherine gasped at the top of a hill, her hand against his forearm. The touch of her fingers through his robe felt like the heat from melted crystal.

She pointed directly in front of him where running north and south, Shadowspawn Mountains blocked their way west.

From high peaks down to steep and craggy slopes, sunlight sparkled on flecks of silver in white rock streaked with black obsidian. Farther down the mountainside, five black obsidian rock formations stood above a black graveled slope like thirty-foot-tall sentinels with carved, dark faces on massive heads. At the bottom of the slope, the sandy road turned north. Serhonydd remembered what he wanted to recall.

"The Gargoyles of Gneiss," he said. "Balsak says that Kylasar turned his five best Black Guards into the Gargoyles to protect his borders."

"You cannot turn men to stone," Wren said as they walked down the road.

"Probably not," Serhonydd said. "But the Gargoyles are made of obsidian, a focal stone for Kylasar's magic. We must be wary. This is Kylasar's domain."

"They remind me of the Easter Island statues," Katherine said, trying to remain calm.

Serhonydd watched her push her auburn hair off her forehead and thought of telling her he loved her. On the road beneath the Gargoyles, Shaeff dropped into a crouch, his ears flicked up and forward.

"What's wrong?" Serhonydd asked. Shaeff raced up the black gravel strewn slope until he reached the closest sentinel. He stopped and sniffed the air.

"What is it?" Serhonydd called.

"I smell something on the wind. More than one," Shaeff responded. And with ears twitching, he cautiously moved forward.

"Dangerous?" Serhonydd asked, moving to take Katherine's arm to pull her close.

An animal's high-pitched braying reverberated through the black-streaked white rocks. Serhonydd scanned the craggy slope above the Gargoyles. And then something screamed with pain. He flinched. *It sounds more human than animal,* he thought.

Katherine recognized the scream for what it had to be. *A child in pain. Mandy!* Suddenly, fear like a cold chill spiked through her. Feet sliding in loose gravel, she raced up the black slope. "Come on!" she cried, and with Shaeff ran into the sentinels' shadows. Beyond the Gargoyles where the mountainside became jagged rock full of dark crevices, she followed Shaeff into a narrow space between two large boulders. Her back brushing the rock and her hands sliding over the rough surface, Katherine finally edged onto the bottom of a dead-end canyon with sides twenty feet high. Thirty feet away, Shaeff stood next to a small, redheaded girl lying on the ground. Disappointed and at the same time glad that it wasn't Mandy who was hurt, Katherine felt guilty. Scrambling to the girl's side, she realized that she could not deny the injured girl the same concern she'd have given Mandy.

CHAPTER THIRTY-FOUR

THE NEEDLEFANG PUNCTURES TRUTH INFECTS ENLIGHTENMENT.

When Serhonydd caught up to her, Katherine was bending over a child sprawled on her back.

"Is it Mandy?" Katherine shook her head.

"No, but she's hurt."

Serhonydd felt a strong pulse behind the girl's ear. Then lifting her head, he found a small lump at the base of the skull. The skin was not cut or bleeding.

"She will be all right," he assured Katherine. He was pleased to see the worry lines around her eyes lessen.

From the rocks above them came a clattering of hooves on rock. Serhonydd turned to see a frenzied donkey crashing and slipping down the steep jagged side of the cliff, its eyes white with fear. Two bloody wounds marked the left foreleg. A Needlefang snake, its venom lethal and very painful, had bitten the donkey. If the donkey did not die from the venom on the way down, its hooves could strike and kill Katherine or the little girl. Serhonydd drew his knife and darted past the crazed animal. He grabbed the donkey's mane and pulled back its head. With one quick move, Serhonydd slit its throat. He stepped back, letting it fall on its left side to the ground, blood spilling over the white and black shale. The donkey rolled its eye up to look at him, raised its head trying to get back up, shuddered, then lay still.

"Crazed from snake bite," Serhonydd said to Wren, who was coming up behind. He wiped the blood from his knife blade in the donkey's pelt. He shuddered from the smell of blood that now seemed to permeate his clothes. He realized that to protect Katherine he had killed the donkey without even thinking.

What if he had had to protect her from a man? Would he have killed a man? *Yes,* he thought. Overwhelmed by the implications, he realized that his parents could have killed those men with swords. So what did it matter that they had used the Power? They had merely used the weapon of their choice. The Power was nothing more than a weapon.

He had spent years avoiding the use of Power, thinking that it would force him to kill. But it could not force him to kill any more than the knife had forced him to kill. He sheathed his knife. His parents had been right. It was time to claim his inheritance.

Wren spoke, interrupting Serhonydd's thoughts.

"The girl was probably riding the donkey when the snake bit it."

Serhonydd nodded. He would worry about claiming the Power later.

"Jorn! I've found Gwenydd!" a voice called from above.

Rock clattered down the slope and above the falling rock, on the back of a donkey rode a little dark-haired girl. Behind her, a man with feathers braided in his long hair rode a horse down the craggy mountainside.

"Oh!" Katherine said. Serhonydd turned to see her standing, white-faced.

"Mandy!" Katherine screamed and scurried up the rocks.

CHAPTER THIRTY-FIVE

O ELEMENTS OF POWER NOW REJOICE, THE CHILDE IS FOUND!

Even as she ran up the mountainside, Katherine wondered why Mandy was traveling by donkey across a strange land with some strange man. Mandy swung down from the donkey and Katherine, her cheeks wet with tears, rushed forward. Then Mandy was running and flinging herself against her mother, and Katherine hugged her hard, kissing her daughter's dirty face.

"I missed you so much!" Katherine cried.

"Come on, Mom," Mandy said, squirming out from under Katherine's arm and grabbing her hand. "I need to see if Gwenydd's all right."

"Gwenydd?" Katherine tried not to slip on loose shale that fell clattering to the rocks below.

Pulling Katherine behind her, Mandy slid down the rock as limber as a mountain goat. "Her donkey pitched her off," Mandy said.

Below them, the feathered man was sidestepping with Serhonydd down the jagged slope of the canyon. When they reached the canyon floor, Mandy raced to the still-unconscious little girl with her head in Wren's lap. Mandy knelt beside her.

"Is she going to be okay?"
"She's fine," Wren answered.

CHAPTER THIRTY-SIX

MANDY'S SAFE; ALL WILL BE WELL, AT LEAST, ALL OUGHT TO BE.

A short time later, after they had sorted things out, Katherine remembered to express her gratitude.

"Thank you for taking care of Mandy," Katherine said to Jorn on the ground next to Serhonydd. Jorn shrugged.

"I was sent to watch over her by the One-Horne."

At the mention of the One-Horne, Serhonydd's eyes darkened to indigo, and Mandy sat up from her mother's lap.

"It's the most beautiful horse I've ever seen!" Mandy said. "Its coat glistened like new snow, Mom, and it had a gold horn right in the middle of its forehead! And look what it gave me!"

From around her neck, Mandy removed a locket and handed it to Katherine.

"Belanos!" Wren interjected. "The Jeweled Locket!"

"May I see?" Serhonydd asked.

The Band of Brocoudahl grew warm around Katherine's forehead, and she knew that only Mandy could allow the necklace to be held by others. Katherine handed Mandy the locket. Serhonydd held his hand out and smiled gently. Mandy hesitated. Katherine could not see her daughter's face and wondered what was being communicated in the silence between Serhonydd and Mandy. Evidently, some decision was made, because Mandy moved to his side. Then she sat down beside him and politely handed him the necklace.

"Katherine," he said. His head bent, eyes fixed on the locket, he said, "Let me see the Key of K'vle, please." She handed it to him.

"See, Mandy?" Serhonydd said. "This is the key that unlocks it."

In order to see better, Mandy bent over, her braid slipping across her shoulder.

"Can we open it, Serhonydd?" Mandy asked.

Wren started to his feet.

"No!" he said. "If you unlock it, then Wry as we know it will be destroyed!"

"You don't know that," Serhonydd replied calmly.

"Let us wait," Wren argued, "and ask the Blue Sorcerers what to do."

Serhonydd's eyes darkened to midnight blue. "That might not be prudent, Wren. Right now we have the Locket and the Key. Kylasar would kill for both, and I am sure that he is looking for us, even as we speak."

"I just want to take Mandy home," Katherine said. She put the Key away.

"How do you propose to do that, Katherine?" Wren asked. "You cannot go back the way you came."

"I don't know ..."

Mandy pulled the chain back over her head and looked up at her mother. "We can go back through the tunnel that Dad and I came here in. It's near Keepsburg."

Serhonydd shook his head. "If it's near Keepsburg, Kylasar would surely find us."

"Then what do you suggest?" Katherine asked him.

"Let me think."

CHAPTER THIRTY-SEVEN

KYLASAR - END YOUR EVIL PLOYS
THE CHILDE IS SAFE IN HAND.

Kylasar had lost what patience he had had. His inept guards couldn't find Mandy. The Rathriders, those elite hounds of Loche, couldn't find Katherine on the mountains, and Jorn, his tracker, had yet to produce the One-Horne. If he wanted the job done right, then he would have to do it himself. It was now time to act.

"You don't seem a bit happy," Loche said.

Kylasar groaned at the god's return.

"Can I be of assistance?"

"Yes, leave."

"Is that any way to treat your friend, your comrade in arms?"

"If you were a comrade in arms, you would help me find Mandy, Katherine, and the One-Horne."

"That's why I'm here. Jorn has forsaken his duty."

"I knew I couldn't trust him."

"He is with Mandy."

"Why would Jorn be with Mandy?"

"Jorn is a traitor. He no longer tracks the One-Horne. Had you been more observant you would have known that, but you have spent your days searching for ways to get rid of me. I wonder if you are a traitor."

"Don't reprimand me, Loche. Without my body, you are nothing but hot air. And, as much as I detest you, I would willingly keep you in my body knowing you want out as much as I want you out."

"Jorn and Mandy are with Katherine."

Before he remembered that Loche was speaking inside his head, Kylasar screamed in rage. "How? Is everyone around me incompetent? Without Mandy, I'll never get the Jeweled Locket from the One-Horne!"

"So take Mandy away from her mother. You did it once. You can do it again!"

Kylasar took the pewter scrying mirror from the mantle. Passing his hand over the glass and whispering Katherine's name, he watched the silvery surface clear to show a steep canyon of white rock streaked with obsidian. On the canyon floor, Katherine and Mandy sat with Jorn and two other men near a prone figure. Kylasar watched Mandy hand a necklace to her mother. Rainbow colors flashed and glittered from gems set on a golden pendant.

"Mandy has the locket!"

"So it seems. They are near the Gargoyles of Gneiss. The Rathriders can bring them here. The locket will be yours to take."

Kylasar smiled. *"I will call in the Rathriders. But after I help you get your corporeal body from the Twisted Plane, you will leave me in peace."*

"You will forego your plan to rule all of Wry?"

Kylasar laughed. *"Never!"*

"Well, in that case, you will probably want my help. Maybe I will stay near at hand."

Kylasar groaned. Maybe if he played his cards just right, he would get rid of Loche, and soon.

CHAPTER THIRTY-EIGHT

O POWERS OF SPIRIT BEWARE, THE RATHRIDERS ARE COME NEAR.

Sitting by Gwenydd later that same evening, Mandy overheard her mother whisper to Serhonydd.

"You don't think Mandy and I can get home, do you?"

"I do not know what to think," Serhonydd said.

Mandy sucked in her breath. She had never thought that she wouldn't be able to go home when her mother found her. She had to go home. All her friends were there. *Except Gwenydd,* Mandy thought, turning to see her friend still asleep. If she went home, she would never see Gwenydd again. Maybe Gwenydd would come home with her, and her mother would adopt Gwenydd. That was it! Gwenydd could be her sister!

"Mom," Mandy said.

Katherine gestured at Mandy to wait, and Serhonydd continued.

"You might be thinking about what to do if you can't go home."

"If I can't go home, how would I manage? I haven't any money to feed Mandy. I couldn't buy a house or clothing. I would not know how to survive. I …"

"Katherine, stop," Serhonydd said quietly.

"I couldn't get a job here. There are no computers."

"Katherine, *stop.*" Serhonydd's voice demanded obedience, and her mother looked dazedly at Serhonydd.

"If we can't find a way for you to return, then I will provide for you, both of you." He looked steadily and strangely at Katherine. *But what did he mean?* She glanced at Katherine, who seemed as confused as Mandy.

"Why?" Katherine asked, her voice a whisper.

Serhonydd's face suddenly flushed and he swallowed. "I care what happens to you, Katherine."

You're in love with my Mom, Mandy thought, *but afraid to tell her!* She held her breath. Did her mother understand, too?

Katherine lowered her eyes, and a smile creased the corners of her mouth. *Even with dirt smudged across her cheek,* Mandy thought, *my mother has never looked as pretty as she did now. Did this mean that she likes him, too?*

Then Katherine stiffened, moved her hands up to that strange, silver band around her forehead, and with a look of horror on her face, she screamed, "Rathriders!"

"Over there!" Serhonydd pointed to a small rock overhang. "Jorn! Leave the horse. Wren, get Gwenydd." He scooped Mandy up under one arm and pulled Katherine toward the overhang. Wren, with Gwenydd over his shoulder and panting, raced toward the overhang, but Jorn, looking more puzzled than scared, stood frozen.

"Come on, Jorn!" Serhonydd shouted. "Rathriders!"

"I'm not leaving Fluke," Jorn said.

Fluke shook her mane and reared. Jorn pulled on the halter, trying to calm the horse. Mandy felt a cold rush of air and a horrible scream echoed into the canyon. Jorn, fighting to hold onto Fluke, was instantly covered with a black shadow. Looking up, Mandy saw a huge bat, its leathery wings snapping like sheets in the wind spiraling toward Jorn. On its back, rode a shape of swirling black smoke with glaring red eyes. Descending, the bat monster dug sharp talons into Jorn's shoulders and blood splattered across the rock. Jorn was yanked up into the air, as another scream echoed off the rock. Then Mandy felt sharp talons tearing her from Serhonydd's grasp.

"Mom!" she screamed into the backlash of wing. Wind that smelled awful, like rotting meat, whipped across her face as the Rathrider carried her higher.

Far below her, bat monsters dropped from the sky like gigantic locusts. *Where is my mother? And where is this bat monster taking me?* The ground was so far beneath her now that through her tears, mountains spread out on her left. A vast forest running the length of the horizon in front of her looked like a thick green rug. Far to her right Jorn, struggling against the talons that held him, twisted around and pulled a knife from his boot. She heard a high-pitched scream and the monster bat jerked its talons back as if something had hurt it. Then Jorn fell free, tumbling end over end toward the trees below.

"Jorn!" Mandy screamed.

CHAPTER THIRTY-NINE

THE POWER OF YOUR NAMESAKE COMES WITH YOUR BECK AND CALL.

Held by a Rathrider, Serhonydd had watched Jorn fall hoping Mandy had not seen it. He felt inadequate. He hadn't been able to protect the little girl or her mother from the Rathriders. Kylasar had still found them. They would not have been in this situation had he taken the Power when his parents wanted him to. He cursed his stupidity. There would be no more senseless deaths. He would take what was rightfully his to protect the ones he loved. Serhonydd closed his eyes. He began his deep breathing and emptied his mind looking deep inside for his inner light. When he found it, he looked through the light to the ground below where he saw a grid of blue energy lines crisscrossing the forest and mountains. Like a fisherman throwing a line into water, Serhonydd threw a thought toward the closest blue energy line and snagged it, and calmly, slowly, drew its energy toward him. He felt electricity raise the hair on his arms and neck and rush down his spine to his feet. Once the Power filled him, he broke the line attached to the energy grid.

From beneath the descending Rathrider, Serhonydd saw Kylasar's castle on a pinnacle of rock. Four main towers higher than the walls were set at the corners with two smaller towers on either side of a massive gate to a wooden drawbridge. Smooth and worn, as if it had been built hundreds of years before, a stone walkway connecting all towers ran the perimeter of the castle.

Kylasar's Keep, he thought and anger flared again. But, now with the Power, Serhonydd could protect them.

CHAPTER FORTY

POWERS OF EARTH, FIRE, WATER, AIR JOIN THE SEEKER AND THE MAGE.

When the Rathrider set Katherine down in a small flagstone courtyard of Kylasar's Keep, Mandy ran sobbing to her mom. From their perches atop three high archways opening onto the western sky, the Rathriders quietly watched with glowing red eyes from atop their bat mounts. Katherine didn't think Eric would harm his own child, but she was not sure. They had to get away.

Flapping wings above her brought Serhonydd, Wren, Shaeff, and Gwenydd, now conscious and crying.

"Where's Jorn?" she whispered to Serhonydd.

"He's dead," Mandy cried. Katherine shuddered, thinking that if Eric had sent the Rathriders, then he was responsible for Jorn's death. But she would not believe the man who had fathered Mandy was the source of evil on Wry. Still, she pulled Mandy close.

Two Rathriders slipped down the walls and pooled their shadow shapes like thick oil on the flagstones. Then from each black pool a tentacle of shadow rose to form a glaring red-eyed Rathrider. They slithered silently forward urging their captives to move beyond the arches onto a square, flagstone balcony enclosed with a knee high stone wall. Beyond and below the wall, Katherine saw nothing but an abyss.

At the edge of the balcony, backlit from the setting sun, black robe flapping like a raven ready to take flight, stood a lone figure. And, although she could not yet see his face, Katherine knew that long and dark red curl of hair along the shoulder, that arrogant stance, that pose long watched in front of a moonlit window. And, as he turned to face the group his dark eyes connected with hers.

"Eric," she said, holding tight to Mandy.

He threw his arms wide.

"Ah, Katherine, at last."

The weeks of frustration tightened her chest and anger flowed like hot molten metal through her veins.

"How could you do this to Mandy? To me?"

"I am her father," he sneered. "I have just as much right to Amanda as you do."

"Not to lock her up!" she said.

"I had to keep her safe. Wry is too dangerous a place for little girls."

"Then why bring her here?" Katherine asked quietly.

Eric put his booted foot on the wall and leaned against his leg. "She is here to help me retrieve a lost object." He smiled absently and rubbed his chin with his thumb.

"And now?" Katherine asked.

"Now?" he repeated, his gaze focusing on her. "She is to give me the locket."

"I intend to take her home with me."

"No," he looked down at his daughter.

Mandy nervously fingered the locket through shirt material. Her father did not look or talk like himself. Her skin broke out in goose bumps. *He is not my father,* she thought.

"Amanda, come here!" Kylasar demanded.

"You cannot force her, Eric," Katherine said, while drawing Mandy close.

"Bring me the Jeweled Locket!" He held out his hand.

Katherine felt the Band of Brocoudahl tingle and grow warm.

Kylasar's face darkened. The air changed as if an electrical storm were suddenly forming, and Katherine felt the hair rise on the back of her neck, thinking she was seeing things. Eric's brown eyes began to glow a phosphorescent, vile green and around the dark edges of his cape at his back, crackling green static flickered. Eric slowly raised his arm and pointed at Gwenydd. From the tip of his index finger, a bolt flashed across the air to enclose Gwenydd in green fire.

Her eyes white with terror, Gwenydd rose inches from the flagstones and flew toward Eric. When she reached his upraised palm, he knocked her to the ground in a heap at his feet.

"Gwenydd!" Mandy cried.

"She's just a child!" Katherine screamed, and then Katherine's inner vision saw past the skin, past the features of Eric's face to a vile corruption. He turned his gaze to Mandy.

"Give me the Jeweled Locket, Amanda, or your friend will find herself tossed like garbage into the abyss behind me."

Mandy ran toward the parapet and in horror, Katherine lunged toward her. Serhonydd's hand restrained her. Mandy stopped and screamed.

"You are not my father!"

From her father's mouth spoke a deep gravelly voice.

"I am Loche, God of Chaos, Father of Despair, and Worker of Destruction, and I will keep your own father's body until you have given me the Jeweled Locket." Loche lowered Eric Kylasar's outstretched hand.

Mandy lifted the chain over her head and gave up the Locket. Loche gestured the green fire away. Mandy helped Gwenydd, sobbing uncontrollably, to stand and then they scurried toward Katherine.

Now Loche lifted the chain above his head and laughed. He took the Locket in hand, turned it over trying to pry it open. But the small Jeweled Locket stayed shut and Loche grew frantic with his failure. With a protective arm around each child, Katherine shuffled backward.

"You!" Loche thundered.

The Band of Brocoudahl seemed to pinch Katherine's head, beads of moisture formed at her temples, and she grew light-headed. She remembered Lady A'legra's words. "Kylasar must battle Kylasar." How wrong the Lady had been, thought Katherine. Kylasar was not Kylasar, but some monster called Loche. And since Kylasar could not battle Kylasar, she told herself, she should be free to leave with Mandy.

"You have what you want," she yelled. "Let us go!"

"Not until I have the Key," Loche said and swept his vile green eyes toward Serhonydd and Wren.

"What Key?" Wren asked, and the green fire flashed from Loche's hand to cover Wren, lifted him high, then dropped him unconscious on the flagstones.

A flash of green lightning split the air. Now Mandy cried out and Katherine whirled in time to see sulfurous smoke envelop her daughter. When the smoke cleared, Mandy was encapsulated in a clear yellow bubble that bobbed noiselessly over the edge of the balcony. Mandy's hands pressed against the bubble and her mouth moved in silent screams.

"Loche! Here's your damn Key, Loche. If you want it, bring Mandy back!" Katherine screamed, fumbling into the pouch for the Key. She feinted toward the balcony's edge, "Or I'll toss it over the edge!"

Loche hesitated, and Katherine's heart dropped into the depths of despair. How could she trust this monstrosity to do the right thing? Then Shaeff, plunging from the darkness behind her, locked his jaw around Loche's leg. The bubble plummeted out and down, and Katherine's piercing scream joined Loche's. Scrambling to the edge of the parapet, Katherine watched the bubble tumble toward the jagged rocks far, far below.

Beside her, Serhonydd pointed at Mandy and a laser-thin filament of blue light from his fingertip raced toward her and enclosed the bubble.

Beside Katherine, Loche screamed again. A crackle of green electricity from Loche's eyes ripped across Katherine, burning her arm. The bubble around Mandy broke and Katherine felt her ears pop from the change in air pressure. Blue light filaments wrapped around Mandy and swiftly, but carefully, Serhonydd, sweat glistening on his brow, drew up the magical line that wrapped Mandy like a blue ball of twine.

Katherine ignored the green electricity sparking over her head as Mandy stumbled over the balcony rail, weeping, and ran into her mother's arms. Serhonydd had already turned to Shaeff, whose jaw still held the screaming Loche.

Katherine, mind spinning with bright, blue light and the Band of Brocoudahl warming against her forehead, stepped toward Loche. Serhonydd, beside her, raised both hands. Blue energy sparked from his fingertips to Loche's temples. A scream that seemed to shatter the eardrums arched his body backward into a heap against the stone wall. A vile green substance poured from his mouth to become a column of foul smoke with lidless eyes, a long snout, skeletal arms, and razors where fingers should be. Katherine shrank back in horror.

This foulness above her was the thing that tried to destroy her daughter. This *evil* was what the Lord Dagda and Lady Brighid had brought her to Wry to fight. And now she understood. She *could* fight Loche and *would* fight to her dying breath any evil that would harm Mandy. Blue light flashed and with her mind's eye Katherine saw the inner light of the power she possessed flare into a furnace of rage.

She *pushed* with her mind. The inner light of power connected with the jewels in the Band and the little flames sprung from the Band to flicker and dance in the air in front of her. The wind whipped around and fanned their flame bodies into a blue-white heat. Then, with a luminescence that was pure and good, they flung themselves at the diabolical creature. Katherine watched them burn through the foul smoke, leaving nothing of Loche's image. Her flame friends then spun back into the Band of Brocoudahl.

Katherine felt Shaeff's gentle mind touch.

"Should I heave him over the balcony?"

"Who?" she asked. Then she saw Eric Kylasar, unconscious and bleeding profusely from a ragged wound in his leg.

"No," she sighed and started to tear the bottom of her shirt for a tourniquet.

A sharp screech drew her attention behind her. Katherine turned to see the Rathriders implode into a dark density that vanished. When she turned back to attend to Eric, he was gone.

"Where's Eric?" she asked Serhonydd.

"Kylasar? According to Balsak, any time Kylasar was defeated by the Blue Sorcerers, he would retreat to the Shadowspawn Mountains to recoup his powers. He will not bother you again, Katherine. However, we Blue Sorcerers will be on our guard. Kylasar will be back."

EPILOGUE

WHEN CRACKS RIP THROUGH REALITY LIFE IS NOT THE SAME.

The following morning, Katherine, Mandy, and Shaeff walked together up the hill to the tunnel where Mandy said her father had brought her from Akron. Serhonydd, Wren, and Gwenydd seemed to lag behind, as if in no hurry to part with the two from Earth, and Katherine was not eager to leave Wren, Shaeff, and Gwenydd. She knew that it would be even harder to leave Serhonydd.

Mandy pointed to an opening in the side of the hill.

"This is it!" She turned to Gwenydd, "Can you come with us?"

"I would be lost on your world, Mandy."

"Mom?" Mandy pleaded.

"She's right, Mandy," Katherine agreed. "We must go back by ourselves." Gwenydd hugged Mandy. Katherine hugged Shaeff and Wren goodbye and then looked at Serhonydd. She wished he would ask her to stay. If he did, then she would, but he merely smiled and nodded at her.

"Serhonydd, you will see that Lady A'legra and Lord A'leron get the Key, the Band, and the Wand?"

"I will."

"And, the Jeweled Locket?"

"Yes. They will do with them as Lord Dagda and Lady Brighid command," he answered.

"Good," Katherine sighed. She took the Band from her head and handed it, sparkling in the sun, to Serhonydd. Then he pulled her to him, kissed her on the forehead.

"Be well," his voice whispered, thick with emotion.

Katherine felt a lump come to her throat. She looked up into his blue eyes and said, "I'll never forget you, Serhonydd."

"Nor I, you."

"It's time to go Mandy." Katherine held out her hand to her daughter, and together they entered the dark tunnel. Mandy held the craerlyte illuminating their path home.

***

A week later, Katherine sat stirring her morning coffee at the breakfast bar. She needed to get dressed for work, but she didn't want to go. It was raining and dreary. Her world now felt black and white, while Wry seemed like a dream filled with color. She missed Shaeff and Wren, and Mandy missed Gwenydd. At night, Katherine dreamed of Serhonydd.

"Mom?" Mandy stopped at the kitchen door, her pajamas still on.

"I thought you were getting dressed for school," Katherine said quietly.

"I don't want to go to school." Mandy whined. "The kids all make fun of me and say I'm crazy and dreamed my dad kidnapped me."

"Don't worry about what they say, honey."

"Will I ever see my dad, again?"

Katherine clinked her spoon again the side of her coffee cup and put it down on a napkin. She sighed. "I don't know."

"I don't ever want to see him again. I thought I'd miss him, but then I remember all the times he hurt you, and I hate him for it." Mandy plopped into a chair.

Katherine leaned over and hugged her daughter. "I divorced your father because I had hoped you would forget about him hitting me." She was sorry that Mandy remembered, but prayed she would forget. When Mandy changed the subject, she was glad.

"I miss Gwenydd," Mandy said, "Can't we go see her?"

"If we were to go back, who's to say we would find her?"

The thought of traveling the land without Serhonydd, Wren, and Shaeff to guide them terrified her.

Lightning crackled and thunder reverberated outside, and Mandy and Katherine both jumped. The kitchen light flickered and, just when someone banged on the kitchen door, the lights went out and plunged the kitchen into a deep black. Katherine, her heart thudding against her chest, called out, "Who's there?"

A sparkle of blue electricity sizzled around the door frame, and as it flew open, blue sparks cascaded like a waterfall across the tile floor. Serhonydd stood in the doorway with his hair and robes drenched with rain. Katherine's heart skipped a beat.

"I've come to take you home, Katherine!"

As if by magic, the lights came back on. Katherine looked at Mandy, and her daughter's bright smile mirrored her own.

LaVergne, TN USA
11 May 2010
182373LV00002B/1/P